UNEXPLAINED LAUGHTER

Recovering from a love affair gone wrong, Lydia retreats to the Welsh countryside, leaving behind her sophisticated friends, but accidentally inviting Betty, 'the human equivalent of sackcloth and ashes'. There they encounter Hywel, a dour farmer, Elizabeth, his nervous wife, the aspiring priest Beuno, Hywel's brother and the randy Doctor Wyn. Meanwhile Hywel's strange sister Angharad roams the land, observing all, while Lydia is increasingly unnerved by the unexplained laughter that comes down from the hills.

UNEXPLAINED LAUGHTER

UNEXPLAINED LAUGHTER

by

Alice Thomas Ellis

Magna Large Print Books
Long Preston, North Yorkshire,
BD23 4ND, England.

British Library Cataloguing in Publication Data.

Ellis, Alice Thomas
  Unexplained laughter.

A catalogue record of this book is
available from the British Library

ISBN   978-0-7505-3758-2

This edition published by Corsair,
an imprint of Constable & Robinson 2012

Copyright © Alice Thomas Ellis 1985

Cover illustration © Diane Law by arrangement with
Constable & Robinson Ltd.

The moral right of the author has been asserted

Published in Large Print 2013 by arrangement with
Constable & Robinson Ltd.

Magna Large Print is an imprint of Library Magna Books Ltd.

Printed and bound in Great Britain by
T.J. (International) Ltd., Cornwall, PL28 8RW

To Jeffrey Bernard
with love

I think I am dead. I think I have been dead for a long time now. I am Angharad. Do you hear me?

Listen.

'…she's only a child, Hywel. She shouldn't be let roam the hills alone.' Elizabeth is speaking. She is Hywel's wife and Hywel is my brother.

She says it again. She says, 'Angharad should not be out on the hills alone. Hywel, she is out on the hills alone…'

He will not answer her. I hear him not answering from where I lie above them with my ear to a hole that the rats made a long, long time ago.

'Anything could happen to her out on those hills alone, anything…' Elizabeth's voice goes with her to the back kitchen. '…you never know who's in the valley these days – strangers.'

She has come back with Hywel's dinner. Hywel is silent and now Elizabeth is silent too. She is as careful as a chemist with her reproaches.

All I hear is the owl, flower-faced, calling once in the night.

'What was that?' asked Lydia. She was standing in blackness in the middle of a narrow, ice-cold stream. The stones over which it flowed were as slippery as its fish and Lydia was wearing town shoes.

'It's an owl,' said Betty.

'No, it isn't,' argued Lydia. 'Owls go tu-whit-tu-whoo. Whatever that was was squeaking. It was a mammal – something furry. Something's eating something furry.'

'Give me your hand,' said Betty irritably. 'I'm on the other side. I think I've found the path again. And it's only the tawny owl who goes tu-whit-tu-whoo. All the rest squeak like that.'

'I can't see my hand,' said Lydia. 'Anyway, you'll have to wait because I'm going to have hysterics. I'm going to stand in this stream and scream.'

Betty had insisted on stopping to eat in a pub, pointing out, with apparent reasonableness, that there would be no cooking facilities ready in the cottage. Lydia had said that one night's fast would be preferable to the plight in which they did indeed now find themselves, but Betty regarded the idea of missing a meal as unnatural and Lydia was overruled. It was during dinner that Lydia had begun to think of Betty as her 'companion' – as the compilers of restaurant guides describe the nameless individuals who share their good fortune and have their meals paid for. 'To start, my companion chose prawns Rose Marie (ugh). Then, for the main course, she chose the steak-and-kidney pie, dripping gravy down her horrible blouse (it's the sort of blouse that when you see it in the shop you wonder how the shopkeeper intends to dispose of it because no one in their right mind would ever dream of swapping cash for it). And you won't believe this, but she rounded off the meal with a wedge of Black Forest gateau. Will she be sick in the car?'

Lydia had never been particularly fond of Betty, but during dinner she had begun to hate her. After dinner they had got lost, because Betty had fallen asleep and failed to note the few signposts and correlate them with the route on the map.

'Did you know,' Lydia enquired, 'that a companion is literally one with whom one breaks bread?' – affectation being as good a means as any of maintaining a distance between oneself and the rest.

'Lydia, for goodness sake come on. You can't stand there all night talking nonsense.' Betty grabbed her and pulled.

'Ouch!' said Lydia, falling in invisible

indignity out of the stream on to her knees.

Betty asked her why she hadn't remembered to bring a torch.

'I think torches are effeminate,' said Lydia. 'I could never never love a man who habitually carried a torch. Could you?'

This was unkind of Lydia, for Betty was not popular with men, which was another reason for Lydia to dislike her, since Lydia was one of those women who find something contaminating in ugliness and prefer to mingle only with those who are at least as attractive as themselves.

She pushed on, dark in the darkness, through barbed and whipping branches to the door of her cottage.

'Now I just wonder if I remembered to bring the key,' she speculated aloud.

'*Lydia*,' said Betty, who was carrying the luggage.

'Oh joy,' said Lydia. 'What an amazing thing. Here it is in my pocket.'

There were candles and matches on a ledge just inside the front door where she had left them on her last visit, for Lydia was in fact a sufficiently practical person and not the ass she sometimes chose to appear.

'Now isn't this cosy,' she observed of the dank and barely furnished room, shadowed in the candlelight. 'There is an old saying that every time an owl hoots a woman has been unfaithful,' she added, lifting the candlestick and looking round.

'There are hundreds of them hooting all night,' protested Betty.

'Yes, well...' said Lydia.

I heard a car stop at Ty Fach. I hear everything in the valley. All the sounds of the valley end here in my room, and the women speak in front of me – of Hywel and Beuno and Elizabeth and me – and the men who work on the farm piss in the hedgerow in front of me because they all think I am dead.

Lydia woke early the following morning and went out to wash in the stream, feeling it was brave and somewhat magnanimous of her after it had treated her so ill on the previous night. Then the icy touch of the water reminded her that she had planned to cool the hock in it for Finn and the bastard wasn't here; and for a moment her towel served as a handkerchief as she mourned, and then, since she considered it degrading to weep for a faithless man, she dried her eyes and her ears and under her chin and returned with springing step to the cottage.

13

Betty was wearing a dressing-gown, a circumstance which served further to upset Lydia, who nevertheless painted her mouth bright red to facilitate her smile and set about connecting the bottled gas to the stove.

Betty, who clearly had not washed, since she had not been down to the stream and there was no water in the cottage, padded about in her dressing-gown and slippers offering to slice the bread for breakfast.

'No, no,' said Lydia, 'don't bother. I'll do it in a minute. We need buckets and buckets of water for washing and cooking and putting in the vodka and down the lav.'

'Oh,' said Betty, but after a moment she went out to the stream leaving Lydia to sit back on her heels and wonder why she found dressing-gowns and slippers so tawdry. By the time Betty returned, her hems wet, she had decided it was because these anachronistic garments dated from an era when there were servants to perform the morning tasks while the quality lounged around in negligé.

'You go and dress while I make the breakfast,' said Lydia, rather too firmly for the perfect hostess. She could not have borne to watch Betty sleazily slicing bread in her dressing-gown. Finn had risen like a god in the mornings, disdaining such suburban embellishments, frying bacon in a state of nature, roaring as the hot fat splattered his ribs.

Lydia had intended to spend the next few weeks alone attempting to eradicate these shafts of reminiscence, determined not to follow the common course and go round seeking replacements for her lost love: an undignified and doom-laden procedure, leading to recriminations and disgust. On several previous occasions she had done this, trying to persuade herself that the new Tom, Dick or Harry was quite as desirable and worthy as the missing Harry, Dick or Tom. It had never proved satisfactory, and as she grew older she was beginning to recognise and make sense of the repeating pattern, like someone unrolling a flamboyant wallpaper. It was at once reassuring and depressing to find life's major events so predictable in their repetition. Eventually, she knew, she would fall in love again. She always did, but it was not a process that could be hurried or engineered. She was not yet prepared to believe herself incapable of what was known as a 'lasting relationship'. She had invited Betty to stay by accident, or rather by drunken mischance, at one of those fatal office parties. She had said, her eyes glittering with simulated enthusiasm, that she could hardly wait to get to her cottage, and Betty had said wistfully that it seemed like years since she had seen a blade of grass (which was silly in itself, because of what else were the lawns of Hyde Park composed?); so Lydia, unhinged with the shock of bereavement, and further undone by wine, had said she could come too. Betty had taken advantage of her weakness, and here she was.

'How do you like your egg?' asked Lydia, determined to be pleasant since the one thing more disagreeable than staying with someone you detested was staying with someone who detested you too. Dissembling was tiring but squabbling was disgusting. She would never be sufficiently intimate with Betty to quarrel with her.

'Poached, please,' said Betty, which was annoying as Lydia had meant hard- or soft-boiled.

Lydia swirled the water in the pan into a whirlpool and slithered in the egg, which proceeded to foam and display other signs of rebellion. 'The bloody thing's stale,' she said.

'They always are,' said Betty resignedly.

At least it didn't stink, thought Lydia. She had been propositioned at that last party by a sub-editor with bad breath, who seeing her maimed and brought down had been swift to seize the opportunity. An egg was very like sex, she reflected. One bad experience could result in life-long egglessness or celibacy. She ladled the flat and listless thing on to a piece of toast and put it before her guest.

I went round the woods behind Ty Fach today. There is smoke in the chimney. Emyr has built it all up and put back the roof. There were bats where the roof used to be before. They hung from the rafters and hardly stirred when I walked beneath. The rafters were green and the floor-boards had crumbled away like old green bread. Ty Fach had been dead for a long time. There are people there now. I shall never go inside Ty Fach again. I think when they steal back the houses they make the earth smaller.

'Was that you in the woods a while ago?' asked Lydia.

Betty stood in the doorway darkening the kitchen as she shook the skirt of her proofed cotton mac. 'No,' she said. 'I just went to the waterfall and back. Though I don't know why I bothered.'

'It does seem rather too much of a good thing – going to look at a waterfall in the rain,' remarked Lydia.

'It wasn't much of a waterfall either,' said Betty.

Lydia considered this rude. She felt proprietorial about the valley. 'It's a very nice waterfall,' she said defensively, adding, in case this ridiculous discussion should end in argument, 'I wonder who was creeping about in the woods?'

Betty looked over her shoulder. 'It was probably the gamekeeper,' she said, 'or a shepherd.'

'Or mad axeman,' suggested Lydia. 'Or maybe it was Nationalists.'

'Oh don't,' cried Betty. 'They burned down a cottage just the other day. Not far from here.'

'They wouldn't get much of a blaze going in this,' said Lydia, gesturing at the rain which was falling in an undisciplined, abandoned way as though someone had forgotten to turn it off.

'I don't know why, if they don't want people to come here,' said Betty fretfully, 'they don't just put up notices all along the border describing the weather conditions.'

'But it is precisely those weather conditions,' said Lydia carefully, 'which make the countryside so unusually beautiful. The depth and particularity of the green are the result of the excessive rainfall.'

She had become aware of a peculiar element in her conversations with Betty. She always paused for rather too long before answering a question or responding to a remark for she feared that if she answered hastily she would say something unseemly.

'Well, there's no point in it being so beautiful if you can't ever go out in it because it's raining,' said Betty, revealing a childish streak in her character which Lydia found rather less appealing than her habitual bossiness. Now she paused so long before answering that she forgot what she was going to say.

Hywel's brother Beuno is coming home. He is my brother too. It is his Christian duty to love me.
  Listen.
I am laughing in the darkness.

The sun shone the next day, and Emyr arrived to connect the water pipes. Betty made him a cup of tea and sat among the cut lengths of gleaming copper and strong-toothed tools conducting a little chat, which afforded Lydia a moment's amusement since Betty was adjusting her conversation to suit a person of low intelligence and the people of the valley were, on the whole, clever, devious and unusually literate. As Betty talked about the rain of the previous days the builder spoke briefly of water tables; as she deplored the unemployment in the Principality he gave a succinct resume of the economic situation; as, somewhat at a loss, she praised the sun for now shining, Emyr described in a few words how it would eventually burn itself out. The scene was rather like a bull-fight, with Betty, small-eyed, blundering hither and yon dazzled by the whisk of scarlet, the glancing slippers of the matador.

'What do you want for lunch?' enquired Lydia when Emyr, having demonstrated that the taps now functioned, had left.

'I thought I'd make us my special salad,' said Betty. 'If you'll wash the lettuce I'll make my special dressing and we could pick some wild sorrel and chop it in at the last minute.'

'Do you know, I'm not hungry,' said Lydia, consideringly. There was something spinsterish in Betty's plans for her salad, something intimate in her expectation that Lydia would collude with her, and some-thing repellent in the prospect of two single women fussing over food in the kitchen. Lydia was damned if she'd play salads with Betty. She felt she might never eat again until Betty had gone. She had real women friends: pretty, witty women more likely to speculate on a swift method of fermenting potato peel than slaver over wild sorrel. Why were none of them here? Because she hadn't asked them, that's why. She had chosen for herself the human equivalent of sackcloth and ashes, and she denounced herself for a masochist. Do I, she asked herself, imagine that because I have lost a man I am in the same category as spotty Betty? Is it my Unconscious (of the existence of which I have informed doubts) that has dropped me in this plight? Because, if so, I had better watch out. 'I think I'll go for a walk,' she said.

'Perhaps it'll give you an appetite,' said Betty.

As she walked, Lydia wondered whether perhaps Betty was lesbianly inclined and that this was why she found her presence so distasteful. After half a mile she had rejected this hypothesis and decided that it was merely because she was unattractive, the sort of person who, fifty years ago, would have worn rubber galoshes. Lydia did not castigate herself for so disliking a fellow-being, believing that it was sufficient merely to refrain from overt unkindness.

The lane had given way to a farmyard.

Lydia skirted it and took to a mountain path which meandered nonchalantly between rowan and hazel trees before stopping to present the traveller with a view of the valley's close. The hill that faced her was bearded like a prophet with a wild white waterfall. The boulders which God had flung about at the time of the creation had, to Lydia's eyes, a patriarchal air, and the pebbles which littered the stream seemed like little children confidently at rest in this fatherly presence. Am I going mad, Lydia asked herself, in her new habit of introspection bred by grief? What is this anthropomorphism, and why do I see this landscape as male? Anyone else would be going on about softly wooded fissures and sweetly mounded hills. I must be careful. She reminded herself that it was not the countryside which had been unfaithful to her and there was no need for her to fall out of love with it.

Lydia sat down on the turf which, in its dry springiness, promptly reminded her of pubic hair. Oh hell, she said to herself and glared morosely at the scene before her, wondering why it was that while, in grief, she could still enjoy a good book or, say, a well-grilled sole, she could take no pleasure in a beautiful landscape. It's the moon-in-June syndrome, she told herself. Lovers clasped, misty-eyed, against a backdrop of hills and trees and water. Soppy cow. She wished that Finn might contract painful boils, and rose to her feet.

A collie, black and white, and twitching strangely, approached her.

'Hi, dog,' said Lydia cautiously, sitting down again. Her imagination, which often inconvenienced her in this way, began to suggest that, naturally, this remote valley would be the haunt of rabid, starving packs of feral dogs.

But the dog was friendly and Lydia was relieved, since there are two sorts of sheep-dog: this sort, and the other sort which bites. There is also a third sort which jumps under motor cars to embarrass their drivers in the presence of the farmer.

Here came the farmer now.

'Hi,' said Lydia, suppressing an urge to apostrophise him by his calling. 'Fine day.'

As rapists never go around with dogs, Lydia's imagination spared her one of its flights. Instead, another regrettable aspect of her personality impelled her to smile specially at this man. She had lost her love, and in her cottage was a woman preparing a possibly sapphic salad; so Lydia gave him the works.

His casual, countryman's demeanour altered perceptibly and he stood still, looking at her.

That's torn it, thought Lydia, swallowing the smile, extinguishing the sexuality which she knew she had caused to flicker about her like burning brandy round the Christmas pudding, and adopting instead a workman-like, country-walking air. She searched for a phrase. Good weather for the crops. Have your sheep been suffering much from the staggers? Have you contributed a great deal this year to the butter mountain? Nothing seemed suitable, and Lydia determined to brush up her knowledge of rural matters and husbandry.

'You at Ty Fach?' he asked.

'Yeah,' agreed Lydia.

'I go by there most days,' said the farmer, proving himself to be the sort of chap who does not mess about but gets straight to the point.

'Oh yeah,' said Lydia gloomily and fell to plucking at the turf between her feet.

'Be seeing you,' said the farmer, giving her a glance of extreme complicity and summoning his dog.

'Not,' said Lydia under her breath and

falling back on the cliché, 'if I see you first.' Then she fell back on the turf and stared at the sky until she deemed it time to go home.

Listen. Elizabeth is lonely. She sighs, and sometimes she hums a little, and then she is silent because she is standing by the window looking out on the yard and turning the rings on her finger round and round. Sometimes the women say she is a saint, but that is only because she has kept me here, and they do not like her. Hywel is rich and they do not like him but he is one of them.

Hywel is crossing the yard. In a moment he will lift the latch and kick the bottom of the door. It used to stick and Emyr has mended it, but Hywel still kicks it.

Elizabeth says in her cheerful voice that will not be cheerful by nightfall, 'I saw the woman from Ty Fach today. She was crossing the yard up to the mountain. She looks quite nice. I might ask her to tea.'

Hywel says, 'Tea.'

And Elizabeth says, 'I might ask her to dinner.'

And Hywel is silent. If he spoke he would say 'Dinner'.

I was up on the hill when the woman came. I saw Hywel speak to her, and after a while, after he had gone, I heard her laugh. She lay on her back and laughed at the sky.

The wind is coming up the valley – quite slowly, like an army that will win.

'Hell,' said Lydia. 'What was that?'

'It's the wind,' said Betty.

Lydia, who knew what it was, exasperatedly poked the fire. 'I hope it doesn't bring the new slates off the roof.' She was not desperately concerned, since she didn't think it would, but it was something to say. She picked up a book and stared at the firelight, hoping that Finn might get bitten by something slightly venomous.

The wind parted imperturbably around the cottage and passed on up the valley. Betty, perhaps carried away by the association of ideas, was talking about flatulence.

'It's caused by a sudden change to a vegetarian diet. The colon is unused to the fibre and it takes some time to adjust.'

'Poor it,' said Lydia. 'I like meat.'

'How you can,' said Betty. 'Just think of those lambs out there. How can you bear to eat them?'

'I don't like lambs,' said Lydia. 'I find them quite unattractive. I like lamb chops.'

'Barbaric,' said Betty.

'Anyway,' said Lydia 'what about that steak-and-kidney pud you had on the way here?'

'There's no meat in pub steak-and-kidney,' said Betty. 'It's all simulated out of woven soya protein.'

'It sounds disgusting,' said Lydia, 'and rather dangerous.'

'Eventually I shall become a vegan,' said Betty. 'No meat or fish or eggs or any milk products at all.'

'Why?' asked Lydia.

'Because it's healthier,' said Betty, 'and it isn't cruel.'

'It sounds to me intensely cruel. If you forced someone to live on nuts and lentils they'd go roaring off to the European Court of Human Rights or something.' Lydia found it remarkable that the people who fussed most about their health with particular reference to diet and exercise seemed rather ill, just as those who enthused most warmly about sexual freedom were rather plain. 'I hate people who go to India,' she said.

'I sometimes think you hate everyone,' said Betty, who would have liked to go round India on a bicycle in an orange robe looking for an Enlightened One.

27

'Not everyone,' said Lydia after a moment's consideration as she worked out the least impolite way of putting what she wished to say. 'Only D.H. Lawrence and Americans and people who call Jane Austen "dear Jane".' She had once heard Betty calling Jane Austen 'dear Jane'. 'I love everyone else except Finn.'

'I can't think what you see in Finn anyway,' said Betty. 'He's got a terrible reputation.'

'I don't see anything in Finn,' said Lydia, who had found Finn's terrible reputation one of his greatest attractions. 'I hate him.'

'I suppose he'd be here now if you hadn't quarrelled,' said Betty with the glancing brutality of those with some intuition but not much intelligence.

'We didn't quarrel,' said Lydia. 'He went off with a lexicographer with cross-eyes and knock-knees and webbed feet – a duck.'

'She had pretty hair,' said Betty, 'and you did quarrel. You were *heard*. Screaming all over Fleet Street.'

Lydia was quite stunned by this. She stared at Betty, her eyes wide, her mouth open: a cartoon of astonishment. 'Who told you that?' she asked, her voice cracked and full of breath she'd been too shocked to exhale.

Betty shuffled a bit. 'Everyone knows,' she said, 'everyone heard you.'

'But I wasn't screaming at Finn,' said Lydia. 'I was screaming at that critic who admires *The White Hotel*. I admit I don't remember much about it, but I do know Finn wasn't there.' True, it was because of Finn that she had got so drunk. She had decided, quietly confident that it was safe to do so, not to accompany him on a tour of some Greek islands, and he had taken instead her of the cross-eyes etc. But the parting had been dignified. She had left Finn, wept commendably few of the scalding tears of blighted love, put a curse on him and her of the knock-knees etc., donned a dashing dress and gone out to dinner. But she *had* got very drunk. She had eaten nothing and towards the end of the evening had smitten the critic across the chest with the length of her arm. She could still feel, from fingertip to elbow, the textures of cotton shirt, silk tie and tweed jacket. Her behaviour had not been normal or good, but it was not Finn she had railed at on the public highway.

'Do you really imagine I'd bellow at Finn in the street?' she enquired. 'I should be mortified if I thought I'd missed a chance to do him a mischief, but it'd be a cold day in hell before I'd make a spectacle of myself in the market place.'

'But you *did*,' reasoned Betty.

'But it wasn't *Finn*,' said Lydia, who could see that Betty, with the facts before her, still preferred her own earlier version and intended to believe it.

This is how history is made, thought Lydia despairingly. Now I'll never dare be famous. I'll never even dare to be successful, because when I'm dead some clod with a thesis to write will put me down as a wild-eyed harridan who jumped on her lover in the street and pulled all his hair out because he'd gone off with a person with webbed feet. There is nothing I can do. If I go on denying it they'll all wag their fingers and say 'Aha' and tell me I protest too much. I shall have to remain here, in obscurity, and rot.

'Why did you get so cross with the critic?' asked Betty with a knowing and unbelieving smile.

'Because the man was a structuralist and an ass,' explained Lydia, 'and you can take that knowing and unbelieving smile off your face.'

'And do you mean you wouldn't be glad if

Finn came back?' asked Betty, economically retaining her expression.

'Of course I'd be glad,' said Lydia. 'If he doesn't come back I shan't get the chance to tell him to stuff it.'

Slowly Betty stopped smiling. After a while she sighed, 'You mean you'd still bear a grudge?'

'Of course I'd bear a grudge,' said Lydia, amazed that anyone could imagine she might not. 'I wouldn't have Finn back if he walked on his head from Mycenae to here.'

Betty ran her finger round the rim of her coffee mug. She looked inexplicably downcast. 'I didn't know you felt like that,' she said.

'Well, why should you?' asked Lydia, puzzled. 'I didn't tell you.'

'No,' said Betty. She got up and shook the cushion on her chair. 'I'll go to bed now. I feel a bit tired. Leave the washing-up for me to do in the morning.'

Lydia opened the door to let out the cigarette smoke and walked as far as the stream, wondering why the blazes Betty was behaving in so singular a fashion. An awful suspicion was growing in her like some bizarre fungus from a tiny spore. What if, she was saying to herself, what if–? But no, it couldn't be. But suppose it was. Suppose Betty had come with her not to gambol on the blades of grass, not to ask her collaboration in salad-making but to keep an eye on her.

And Lydia knew it was so. Betty was here out of the kindness of her heart to minister to a wounded human being; Betty would probably rather be in the Dordogne, but she was here making sure that Lydia didn't lay violent hands on herself in the profundity of her misery, or let herself go to seed in the spiritless fashion of an old thistle.

Lydia emitted a sudden giggle, helpless to prevent it. She wished she could stand in the night and laugh, but already she had been heard. A shrew scuttled away in the undergrowth and Betty had opened her bedroom window wider.

'I'm just coming,' called Lydia, thinking how amusing it would be to make a big splash and drowning noises, but even she knew that this would not be the action of a nice woman.

'In a week,' says Elizabeth. 'Beuno is coming in a week's time. I must fill the freezer.'

Hywel is silent.

'I must think of some things for him to do,' says

Elizabeth. 'I must plan some parties.'

Hywel is still silent. He is thinking that Beuno had lived here all his life and no one thought of things for him to do, or gave parties for him before. I know what Hywel thinks always. I can read his silence.

'I'll ask the woman from Ty Fach,' says Elizabeth in the voice that she uses to make promises, 'and the girl who is staying with her.'

'Ask who you like,' says Hywel, and then says no more.

But this time the silence belongs to Elizabeth.

Lydia woke late the following morning. She could hear Betty reigning below in the kitchen, shuffling plates and boiling water, and doubtless adding some original touches to the toast: slicing it laterally perhaps, or dusting it with cinnamon. She felt the desolation of a child in a strange house, saddened by the alien nature of the sandwiches, bewildered by the peculiar quality of the trifle which the family of the house take greedily for granted, almost afraid of the unfamiliar shape of the jelly, choked by the frogspawn lump of unshed tears, past which not one small sweetie can negotiate a passage. Yet she had watched unmoved as Finn put strawberry jam on his mutton because there was no red currant jelly. She supposed that marriage must be like that: an unquestioning acceptance of the weird ways of another. Lydia was resigning herself to a long stretch of celibacy. She couldn't even eat with people she didn't like, and as for sleeping with anyone – unless she was wildly in love or pissed out of her mind she couldn't do it. And when she was drunk she snored. Never, in all her life, had Lydia gone to bed with anyone out of simple mechanical need and never out of the kindness of her heart.

When she came downstairs Betty was sitting at the table.

'You must be starving,' she said. 'You ate nothing yesterday.'

'I'm not,' said Lydia. 'I'm not hungry at all.' Betty had a greasy crumb on her chin. Lydia didn't know whether or not she had washed her hands. Her frock was unironed.

'I'm going to make you a buttered egg,' said Betty decisively, rising to her feet.

'I'm not going to eat it,' said Lydia. 'I'll have a cup of coffee.'

'You'll be ill if you don't eat,' said Betty. 'You'll get run down and depressed.'

'No, I won't,' said Lydia. 'I never eat if I'm not hungry, and when I'm not hungry for long enough I get gloriously high. After a bit I'll probably start seeing visions. You should know that. Fasting makes one mystical.'

'It makes one dead after a while,' said Betty, taking the practical line. 'No matter how unhappy you are you must eat.'

Dear agony aunt, said Lydia in her head, I have a person staying with me whose presence disinclines me from food. She thinks I am pining away from love. How do I put the truth to her?

Dear Lydia, said her head, you are clearly a very neurotic woman. Seek help.

She said aloud: 'I'm really not unhappy. When I'm really unhappy I eat chocolate and raw bacon and sleep by the fridge.' This wasn't true, but Lydia knew that some people did.

'Well, put a lot of milk in your coffee,' said Betty, sitting down again.

Someone outside the kitchen door said, 'Hello.'

'Oh hell,' echoed Lydia, putting her cup down.

'Come in,' called Betty, quite the lady of the house.

Really I can't stand it, thought Lydia. I'll have to get rid of her. She's feeling what she thinks I should feel and she's living my life.

She's making me inhuman. She's turning me into a wild animal. Soon I shall start snarling at visitors and grubbing for nourishment in the fields, simply because I cannot bear to think of myself in the same category as Betty, and *she* has laid claim to humanity. She is going to go on behaving beautifully and so I shall be forced to behave like a pig to establish the difference between us. I wonder how far this necessity explains many criminal and anti-social acts. Was it the blameless wonderfulness of God that forced Satan to go and live in the pit, where he could leave his things lying around and put his feet on the table?

'Get rid of whoever it is,' said Lydia in a hiss, slithering swiftly up the stairs. She shut her bedroom door, knowing fate had decreed that the book she was reading should be resting in the sitting-room, leaving her with nothing to do but make her bed, sit on it, lie on it, unmake it, jump on it, push it round the floor – there were limits to what you could do with a bed, and it was the only piece of furniture in the room. Or she could kneel and look out of the window, or do some physical jerks. She swung her arms above her head and cracked her hand on a low beam. 'Ow,' she said.

'Lydia,' called Betty. 'What are you doing? We've got a visitor. Come down.'

Lydia stared incredulously at the floor-boards through which these words rose. She couldn't call back that she was asleep or had died.

'This is Elizabeth,' said Betty as Lydia walked into the kitchen, wearing grey. Her clothes could not be described as unsuitable for the country, but they were not the sort of thing a country woman would wear. Elizabeth in a print frock looked very much more utilitarian than Lydia in her shirt and trousers.

'Hi,' said Lydia uncompromisingly.

Betty looked at her apprehensively. 'She comes from the farm at the top of the valley,' she explained.

'Oh yeah,' said Lydia, beginning to feel mad. It was surely only people of diminished responsibility who found their lives being taken over in this way. Being unmarried and childless she was unaware that many quite normal women spent a great deal of time talking to and feeding people whom they would not, themselves, have chosen to enter-tain. It seemed insanely silly to Lydia that she should be standing in her own kitchen flanked by two women for whom she had no time. She thought of the people she liked, whose company she enjoyed. Not one of them could be described as ordinary. Lydia played only with court cards. Her friends were mostly interestingly self-destructive: drinking, and smoking, and embarking on disastrous relationships. Their clothes were expensive and had cigarette burns in them, their licences had been taken away from them, their faces showed signs of what is known as the ruins of great beauty, they were always in various stages of depression; and, being the way they were, this had the effect of making them exceedingly witty with the scaffold humour that Lydia preferred. Few of them were caused by melancholy to sit staring slackly into the middle distance. As their sorrow increased so they grew bolder. Lydia thought of her dear ones whirling in their merry dance of death, their faces pale, their bright eyes wild, the tips of their cigarettes gleaming in the tumbling, roaring gloom... At this point she accused herself of exaggeration and made some boring remark about the countryside.

'Aren't you frightened to be here alone?' asked the visitor.

'No,' said Lydia, not entirely truthfully. Sometimes she rehearsed in her mind means of escape from the murderer who lurks always just within the consciousness of the solitary. As he crept in through the scullery window she would leap from her bedroom and conceal herself in the nettles, unconscious of the pain. As he climbed through her bedroom window she would flee down the stairs, slamming the door on his sanguinary hand. But when she was very sad she understood that sorrow casts out fear, and then the murderer could call with a few of his friends and she would tell them wearily to bugger off and they would go, since, after all, there can be no satisfaction in murdering the dead. Sometimes Lydia felt that she had very little to lose, and in her poverty lay her safety. 'No,' she said again with more conviction.

'I'm giving a dinner party,' said Elizabeth to Lydia with the odd composure of those who are conversationally inept and unaware of it. 'On Thursday.'

'Why *should* we be frightened?' asked Betty, nervously.

'Oh, I should be,' said Elizabeth. 'At the farm I have the dogs and...' she paused, 'no one comes much to the farm unless I ask them specially.' She got up and moved towards the door. 'You should lock the doors and windows at night,' she advised them.

'I always do,' said Lydia when she had gone. 'Was she asking us to her dinner party? Or was she just telling us she's having one because she thought we might be interested?'

'She'd already invited us before you came down,' said Betty. 'What do you think she meant about locking the doors?' She looked behind her apprehensively.

'I suppose she meant we should lock the doors,' said Lydia, adding meanly, 'Of course we are particularly vulnerable here. Anyone who really wanted to could get in with no trouble at all.'

'Oh don't,' cried Betty. 'You're making me nervous. I wish we had a man with us.'

'If we did he might be the murderer,' said Lydia. 'Finn had violent tendencies. I laughed at his coat once and he pushed me off a bar stool.' She found it comforting to remember sometimes the worst aspects of Finn's behaviour.

'Well, no wonder he went off with that girl,' said Betty.

'Huh,' said Lydia. She wished that Finn's caique might sink in waters infested with small sharks. She hoped that one might eat the duck with the lovely hair. 'I'm going down to the pub,' she said; 'I need a drink,' and added rather threateningly, 'You coming?'

'I never drink in the daytime,' said Betty. 'It makes me go to sleep in the afternoon.'

It made Lydia go to sleep in the afternoon too, which was why she did it. She was frustrated by the unsatisfactory nature of the recent conversation. She found Elizabeth hard to place, her personality oddly opaque, her responses subdued and elusive. 'Is that girl half-witted, or is it me?' she enquired.

'What do you mean?' asked Betty.

'Being a communicator,' explained Lydia, 'I find it dashed annoying not to be able to communicate.'

'You don't communicate really,' said Betty. 'You just like telling people things. You don't expect a response.'

'Of course I do,' said Lydia. 'I wouldn't fancy just standing there yelling into the void.'

'You like people to respond by telling you how clever you are,' said Betty. 'That's not actually a response. It's flattery.'

Lydia felt quite breathless. Betty was being rude to her. How extraordinary. Every worm has a turning. 'If they didn't read what I write I should starve to death,' she said.

'You could do something else,' said Betty. 'But you wouldn't feel real if you weren't surrounded by people most of the time telling you how wonderful you are. I'm not blaming you. Some people are simply just like that.'

'I'm not like that,' said Lydia, but she wondered. Betty didn't sound as though she meant to be unkind. She sounded as though she was stating a fact. How very unpleasant it can be, she reflected, to see oneself as others see one. Is it preferable to be a rat or a mouse – a long-tailed, snaggle-toothed, terror-inspiring rat or a little grey domestic pest? On the whole, she decided, being a rat was more *chic*, but nevertheless she determined to write a long earnest article soon on some subject of profound importance in which she would make a significant contribution to the sum of human awareness. Betty's fond tolerance was not enough. Lydia wanted her respect. How greedy. 'Anyway,' she said, 'I *am* off to the pub. Here I go.'

'They'll think you're an alcoholic,' warned Betty. 'You know how people talk in these small communities.'

'I am an alcoholic,' said Lydia. 'And they mostly talk in Welsh and I don't understand them, so I don't care. The day they come to the door and denounce me in fluent Anglo-Saxon for a Scarlet Woman, then I'll think about it.'

When Hywel went to the hills Elizabeth went to the telephone. She said, 'Come to my dinner party', and she said 'Why not?', and she said, 'Beuno will be here and the Molesworths are coming, and I've asked the two girls who are staying at Ty Fach.' She said, 'April can't come. It's her evening class in Oswestry', and she said, 'About eight o'clock. Come as soon as surgery closes,' and when she turned from the telephone she smiled.

That night a storm circled the valley. The watchful, who included Lydia, watched the sky behind the hills lurid with lightning and heard the distant cursing of thunder. What a scene, thought Lydia, who was a connoisseur of rows. The lightning flashed with bitter, brief, revealing wit, and the inarticulate thunder grumbled, protested and eventually roared. The lightning replied and then at last retired leaving the dull thunder the last fading word. And the night wept heavy, despairing, relentless tears.

'Wow,' said Lydia, heaving herself to the

other side of the bed and plumping up her pillow. She remembered uneasily one or two scenes with Finn, and wondered whether, in battles with a loved one, it might not be advisable to suppress the cutting edge of one's cleverness. The lightning, it seemed to Lydia, had undoubtedly come off best in that encounter. If she were the thunder, she thought, she would never speak to it again.

Next morning, the countryside was heavy and sullen like a house where a dreadful quarrel has taken place and still nothing is resolved. A dark palpable mist hung over the moorland and behind it the sun flamed in temper.

It was a lousy day. Everybody said so. Lydia and Betty said so, and when Lydia went into the village shop it was full of people who were saying so as well. It was the sort of day when men run their fingers round their collars and women pull their skirts away from their thighs, and people debate whether a hot cup of tea really cools you down or whether a glass of cold water is more helpful. 'It's so humid,' they moaned, and they wondered why it was that the storm had left them in this stifling, steamy condition when storms were supposed to clear the air. Even the older villagers claimed they'd never known anything like it. Some who had driven over the Berwyns insisted that they had had to put their headlights on, and this in the middle of a July day.

After a while Lydia grew bored with hearing people insulting the weather. Contrarily, she determined to find something to say in its favour. It was, after all, an unusual day, with its ominous dark mist. It made the previous days seem like shallow, callow girls, all light and bright and ordinary. 'It's not such a bad day – sort of interesting,' she said. It was now that she gained her reputation for eccentricity. Being an outsider she would have got it anyway, but this precipitated matters.

'Oh, you like it, do you?' asked an elderly farmer, buying a quarter of boiled ham for his tea. 'Well, well, then.'

That seemed to sum it up, and Lydia left for home, driving slowly because of the sheep, the young pheasants, the occasional rabbit and the small groups of tourists on their way to view some antiquity or item of rustic charm who variously loped, flapped, skittered and scuttled before her. She stopped at the graveyard to visit the dead; but as, even alive, they would all have been strangers to her she felt intrusive. It was not correct, she thought, to walk among these sleepers, regarding their bed-heads wrought from stone and criticising their counterpanes of gravel. The grass-grown graves looked the most comfortable. There was something uneasy, something that still protested, in the others – the ones with the polished granite headstones and low-walled rectangles of tooth-white, glittering chippings – as though the occupants lay open-eyed, indignant at their powerlessness to alter their unjust circumstances. These, felt Lydia, would rise on the last day, climbing briskly out of their coffins, brushing away the mould of corruption and muttering, 'About time too.' They would instantly begin questioning the way the world had been running since their enforced absence, and they would not approve; whereas those who lay softly beneath the blowing grasses, the quiet slate, had long since turned over in rest and when they woke would wake like children and smile at the sky. Lydia's imagination was at it again. She thought she ought to be able to master it sufficiently to make it write a poem for her, but it didn't work like that.

There was someone else in the graveyard; someone who slipped soundlessly behind the church as she watched.

That's a ghost, said Lydia's imagination.

'No, it isn't,' said Lydia. 'It's the village idiot.'

She left the car outside the churchyard in a space where the cockpit used to be and walked home.

Betty was sitting in the porch of the cottage peeling potatoes. The porch was made of slate like the peaceful gravestones. It was economical, thought Lydia, and reassuring to make your dwelling place of the same indigenous material as your grave. Living and dying here you would feel much the same.

'I saw the most extraordinary creature in the churchyard,' she said.

'What sort of creature?' asked Betty suspiciously, possibly thinking of those large mysterious cats which are regularly sighted all over the British Isles but never caught.

'I think it was a girl,' said Lydia. 'She didn't look quite human.'

'Oooh, you are horrible, Lydia,' said Betty indignantly.

'I don't think all that much of humans,' said Lydia; 'so when I say one doesn't quite look like one I don't mean it offensively.'

Betty found this rather hard to understand, and Lydia sounded dangerous, so she peeled another potato.

Appeased by the silence, Lydia went on: 'She looked at home in the graveyard. More at home than the ladies in hats who come on Sundays with chrysanthemums...' She was thinking that the girl might have lacked an umbilicus; might have come straight from the hand of God, who having finished making the mountains had picked a bit of clay from under his thumbnail and fashioned just one more sort of person, perhaps as an experiment. Naturally she didn't say this. Some thoughts are entirely unsuitable for conversation. 'Most people are like plates,' she said instead; 'so if one gets broken you can go back to the shop and get another one of similar pattern.' But that made her think of Finn, who really wasn't much like other people at all. 'I shall never own anything of value,' she said. 'Things of value are death to peace of mind.'

'Do cheer up,' said Betty.

'No, I won't,' said Lydia. 'This is not a day for cheering up on. This is a day for thinking of the Four Last Things and meditating on sin.' She had forgotten her brief attempt to enjoy it, and looked round at it with disgust. It made her think of sour washing.

I saw the woman from Ty Fach today. She was

in the graveyard. Some of the people read the gravestones as they read the addresses on envelopes. The woman looked at the graves as though she would like to open them. She looked at the grave of Hywel's mother. One day I shall lie beside that grave and the stone will say 'Angharad' and I shall have been dead for a long time. She was my mother too.

Betty wrought all those peeled potatoes into *rosti,* and grilled some sausages, remarking that they contained very little meat. She was frustrated by the narrow range of vegetables available in the country and said that tomorrow she would go foraging in the fields for different types of mushrooms and wild herbs. She was missing the aubergines and things that brightened the street-markets of London and was discommoded by the absence of garlic. The nearest town was sufficiently far north to be a pie place, and nearly all the shops – the butchers, the bakers, the grocers, the solitary delicatessen – vied with each other in the quantity and variety of their pies. And certainly they took a casual attitude to vegetables, clearly regarding them as very second-rate fodder and not really to be taken seriously. Betty was horrified to note that the butchers' shops kept cooked pies adjacent to raw meat. 'The risk of salmonella,' she said, 'the possibility of food-poisoning. Oh! Are none of them aware of the dangers? I wonder what the health inspectors are thinking about.'

Lydia felt some sympathy with Betty for once. Now that she knew Betty was here because she pitied her and not because she liked her, she felt less threatened and decided that she would just let her take over the cooking and do as she wished in the kitchen.

'I've got to work on some stuff for an article,' she said. 'I'll take it up to my bedroom and you can listen to the radio in the sitting-room.'

'I thought I'd sit in the garden,' said Betty. 'The mist's nearly cleared and I like to see the stars.'

'What a good idea,' said Lydia.

She lay on her bed and after a while heard Betty come in again, slapping at her cheeks and arms. Lydia grinned. She could have told her guest that the midges were like little piranhas of the air; but she hadn't, and now Betty had found out for herself.

Behaving badly made Lydia feel better. She hoped she wasn't turning into one of those maniacs who murder people in order to establish their superiority over their fellows who say Please and Thank you and conform to the basic customs of society. She thought it unlikely. Murder seemed to her too intimate, too similar to giving birth. She thought she would never care enough about anyone to give birth to them or to kill them. With the possible exception of Finn. Lydia lay for some time wondering how best to upset him. The duck with the hair was not unlike Betty, which was probably why Betty found her so attractive. It was something to do with their hemlines, mused Lydia: something to do with the length and disposition of the bottoms of their skirts. They both sometimes wore white stockings, which compounded the uniquely maddening quality of their hems, adding to the aspect, both prim and clinical, which so infuriated Lydia. They were no better in trousers, because then they both got the waistline wrong. Spinsters should never even attempt to marry, thought Lydia drowsily, and fell asleep.

She woke a short while later under the impression that she'd dropped off at a cocktail party. She had heard people laughing. The room was nearly dark and the silence unbroken.

She got off the bed and listened. Perhaps

Betty had asked some people in and they were enduring one of those breaks in conversation, but the silence went on. By now two people would have started talking at the same moment. She went downstairs.

Betty was quite alone reading a book called *Yarns of an Old Shellback* that Lydia had brought from her father's house.

'Who was laughing?' enquired Lydia abruptly.

Betty stared at her. 'No one,' she said.

'Someone was,' said Lydia. 'It woke me up.'

'It must have been the wind in the trees,' suggested Betty.

'Winds roar and howl and occasionally whisper,' said Lydia, 'but they don't, to the best of my recollection, laugh.'

'Then it must have been the stream running over the rocks,' said Betty.

'And while I know streams are said to chuckle,' remarked Lydia acidly, 'they don't go like this – Har Har Har.' She gave a mirthless impression of a full-bodied laugh.

'Then it must have been a ghost,' said Betty, and clearly wished she hadn't. 'There's no such thing as ghosts,' she affirmed.

'I think there probably are,' said Lydia argumentatively. 'Only I can't see what they've got to laugh about. On the other hand, now I come to think of it I can't see why they should go round clanking chains. What a waste of time. If I was dead I think I might laugh. After all, death frightens the hell out of everyone; so once you'd gone and got it over with you might feel quite light-hearted.'

'You mean nothing worse could happen?' asked Betty doubtfully,

'Yeah,' said Lydia.

'But what about reincarnation?' asked Betty.

'I don't know about reincarnation,' said Lydia, 'except it sounds to me a bit of a dirty trick. You think you've got it all over with – and bang, you're re-cycled as a beetle or something. Anyway, just at present I'm thinking about disembodied laughter.'

'Was it – frightening?' asked Betty.

Lydia thought, 'It wasn't at the time,' she said, 'because I didn't know it was inexplic-able. I'm not frightened now. It wasn't a lunatic giggle. But I wouldn't go outside at the moment.'

'Oh, we are silly,' said Betty, straightening up in her chair.

'It must've been someone walking home from the pub.'

'Can't have been,' said Lydia. 'If they were on the road we couldn't hear them from the house, and I truly doubt that anyone would go home via the graveyard and the woods. And if they did they wouldn't be laughing; they'd be too busy tracking their way through the undergrowth. Besides, the only people who live beyond here are that Elizabeth and the farmer, and neither of them strikes me as the riotous type.'

'Then it must have been holiday-makers out for a walk,' said Betty.

'I suppose,' said Lydia, but she somehow knew it wasn't.

There was a storm and it stayed. It lay in the valley all day like a dead body and I didn't go out. I lay in my room like a dead body and I listened to Elizabeth thinking about her dinner party.

She opened her cookery book, and after a while she boiled a chicken, and she sang.

Beuno is coming home today, and tomorrow is Elizabeth's dinner party, and Dr Wyn will come.

Elizabeth is going to be very kind to me.

Lydia and Betty were the first to arrive and were met by two of the farm dogs – one charming, one not, like pairs of detective inspectors. Lydia had an impression when Elizabeth opened the door that no one had spoken in that house for some time. She then thought that people seldom visited here, and yet Elizabeth was not an incompetent hostess. She took them through the square hall into a sitting-room and offered them sherry. She was not shy, but neither was she easy. After a while Lydia understood. She had herself spent several weeks alone in her cottage when she had just bought it and when she returned to mix with people she had found that her vocabulary had deserted her, that without stimulation she had completely lost the art of conversation, had been able only to mutter inanities in monosyllabic form. It had soon passed, but it had alarmed her at the time. It was not pleasant to feel like a mindless bore.

'Have you always lived here?' asked Betty.

'No,' said Elizabeth. 'My parents bought a bungalow and retired down here and I met Hywel and married him.'

Lydia thought that this statement lacked joy.

Obviously Betty thought the same. 'How lovely to live here permanently,' she observed brightly. 'Such a wonderful spot for children.'

55

'I haven't any children,' said Elizabeth.

Betty rallied. 'Oh, you will have,' she promised. 'I know you will.'

How do you know, wondered Lydia, her thoughts taking on an indelicate hue.

Elizabeth said nothing, and Lydia judged it her turn to speak.

'Do you know if Ty Fach is haunted?' she asked.

'Oh *Lydia*,' said Betty.

'I think these old places always have ghosts,' said Elizabeth as though she were talking of woodworm.

The girl is depressed, thought Lydia. Most people grew animated at the mention of the supernatural, whether they believed in it or not. She felt that a whole phalanx of gibbering wraiths could rise from beneath the flagstones and Elizabeth would indifferently offer them sherry. There was something funny here, and Lydia suspected that it was not the sort of funniness that she would enjoy.

Outside, the bad dog recommenced barking rather savagely as a car drew up in the yard. Elizabeth waited for a moment as though for someone else to open the door and then rose and went to do so herself.

'What do you think?' whispered Betty,

leaning forward towards Lydia and indicating the room.

'What about?' asked Lydia in normal tones. Whispering about people when they had left the room was one of the naughty things she didn't do.

'Sssh,' went Betty, sitting back as Elizabeth returned with another guest.

'Wyn,' said Elizabeth. 'He's our doctor.'

'How do you do,' said everyone.

Lydia was finding it increasingly difficult to place Elizabeth. Her own grandfather had regarded doctors as tradespeople and would not have dreamed of asking one to dinner, but most people below the rank of bank manager treated doctors with awe and respect, calling them 'Doctor' all the time. Elizabeth didn't. She behaved as though she was rather bored with this one, as though she knew him very well and yet had little use for the knowledge. Had he made a pass at her, wondered Lydia?

She was wearing her scarlet silk. Its message ran like this: 'This is my best frock. If you lay a finger on me, you little squirt, you'll crease it, and if you do I'll kill you.' The doctor had misread the message and clearly imagined she was wearing it to entice. He was looking at her as though she were for sale.

'Where's Angharad?' he asked. 'She usually lets me in these days.'

'She'll be in her room,' said Elizabeth, 'or wandering round the hills. I've tried and tried to bring her out, but she's slipping back.' She sounded discouraged.

'You did wonders with her,' said the doctor. 'Don't worry about it.'

'Who's Angharad?' asked Betty, to Lydia's surprise and regret. It was so obviously a tactless question.

'She's Hywel's sister,' said Elizabeth. 'She's not normal.' There was something spiteful in her words, something bitter and punitive. Quickly, but too late, she added, 'Poor child.'

The doctor said something incomprehensible about Angharad's medical condition, and Betty praised a corner cupboard of Welsh oak which stood adjacent to the window.

'Where's old Hywel, then?' asked the doctor. 'Running round after his sheep?'

'He'll be in soon,' said Elizabeth, sounding unconvinced. She added with more assurance that Beuno would also soon return from his walk to the waterfall, and then wondered aloud where the Molesworths were, because in a minute they would be late.

'Quite a party,' remarked the doctor as the

58

barking began again in the yard.

'That'll be them,' said Elizabeth, going out.

A middle-aged couple entered the sitting-room, and Elizabeth could be heard in the hall bidding someone go and change.

'Hullo there,' said the doctor, greeting them as old acquaintances and introducing them to Lydia and Betty.

After a brief, appalled glance at Lydia, Mrs Molesworth (Lil) sat down on a corner of the sofa and asked the doctor a question about the imminent agricultural show designed to exclude Lydia from the conversation, to reveal her close knowledge of this event and therefore to illustrate her important position in the local community. This was because Lydia's red frock bore another message, which went: 'This red frock is more chic and expensive than anything which you possess, and it makes you look a provincial old trollop in your mock Chanel suit.' Mr Molesworth (Sid) was also intimidated by Lydia and allied himself with his wife's question.

'Lil and Sid were my parents' oldest friends,' explained Elizabeth, standing and pouring sherry.

'Both her parents died a couple of years back,' said Mrs Molesworth in an aside to

Betty. 'Very sad.'

'Oh, that is sad,' said Betty.

Elizabeth looked consciously unmoved, as though someone had paid her a compliment which, in modesty, she must affect not to have heard.

'They were such nice people,' said Mrs Molesworth. 'We do miss them. He'd only just retired, and they'd built a beautiful bungalow.'

'Where do *you* live?' enquired Betty, contriving to look at once serious, since the subject had been death, and also interested in the Molesworths' continuing existence. This is very difficult to do, and unless the practitioner is careful she ends up resembling the Prime Minister feigning compassion in the face of some disaster. Lydia found her irritating.

'In the house behind the garage,' said Mrs Molesworth, looking faintly surprised, as might the Queen on being posed that question. 'We run the garage, you know. And the gift shop.'

'Oh yes,' said Betty nervously. Lydia had been eloquent about the house behind the garage.

'We had it built to our own specifications,' said Mrs Molesworth. 'We always promised

60

ourselves we'd do that one day – have everything just the way we wanted it.' Her voice had the overtones of gentility which only Northerners seem able to achieve.

'Where do you come from?' asked Betty with an eye on Lydia.

'We came from the North,' said Mrs Molesworth, making herself sound like a Viking horde. 'We used to holiday here and we always promised ourselves we'd live here one day.'

'How lovely,' said Betty inadequately.

Lydia was twirling her sherry glass and peering into it thoughtfully.

Betty attempted to steer the subject clear of building. 'Don't you find it awfully cold in winter?'

'Oh, we have under-floor central heating,' said Mrs Molesworth complacently. 'Even in the kitchen. We've got a white Italian marble floor in the kitchen. I don't like open fires. They make such a lot of work.'

'Yes, don't they,' agreed Betty desperately.

Lydia, still twirling-her glass, was lying back in her chair and regarding her unblinkingly.

Don't say a word, implored Betty silently, gazing back at her.

This is going to be a very wonderful evening, thought Lydia, polishing off her sherry. But in the end it was all right because of Beuno.

'Well, thank God for Beuno,' said Lydia as they drove home in the dark. 'I thought for a moment there I was going to get hysterical and start yelling knickers. I don't think I've ever come across anything quite so refined as Lil. Unless it was Sid. I don't think I ever met a refined man before. It's a very peculiar sensation. Then I nearly fell over when Hywel walked in because I met him on the mountain and he gave me the eye.'

'He didn't seem too delighted to see you,' said Betty.

'No, he didn't, did he,' said Lydia thoughtfully.

'I liked Beuno,' said Betty.

'So did I,' said Lydia, surprised. When Beuno had come in the tension had eased. 'Without Beuno,' she observed, 'that evening would have been impossible. Hywel was glaring mad at having to put a suit on. Lil and Sid hated me like rat poison...'

'That was your own fault,' interrupted Betty. 'You were so rude to them. When she said they'd just been to see their son in Rhodesia and you said "Kenya for officers, Rhodesia for other ranks" it was *awfully* rude.'

'I should have said Zimbabwe,' said Lydia. 'That would've made them even madder. Weren't they horrible?'

'Oh *Lydia*,' said Betty, 'they were just perfectly nice, ordinary people.'

Lydia shuddered. Betty had embarrassed her exceedingly because, seeing that the Molesworths were dismayed and repelled by Lydia's uncompromisingly exotic appearance, she had explained that Lydia was a most brilliant journalist. She had gone on and on about it until Lydia's face had ached from grinning in appreciation of Betty's praise and frowning in polite dismissal of her wilder flights. The Molesworths had been impressed, but as they never read the various journals for which Lydia worked they were little the wiser. Lil had said, 'I always think it must be so nice to be able to write.' And Sid had said, 'If I had the time I could write down some of the things I've seen that you wouldn't believe.'

Lydia could still feel her hands sweating.

'And I don't see,' continued Betty, 'why you had to say Elizabeth was going up and down like a whore's drawers when she was only moving things off the table.'

'She did an awful lot of it,' said Lydia. 'She

was making me hysterical. I was getting giddy. Up, down like a...'

'And there was no need,' said Betty, gathering momentum, 'to tell that poor woman what *orchid* means.'

Lydia, who was still too drunk to feel repentance, slid lower in the driver's seat, limp with remembered mirth. *Orchis* is Greek for testicle, which is what the roots look like, and Lydia had told the company so, because Mrs Molesworth, gazing fondly and favourably on her husband, had divulged that he had bought her orchids on the recent occasion of their wedding anniversary.

'Anyway,' said Lydia, sitting up, 'it was Beuno who went on about the golden emerods.'

'That was your fault too,' said Betty. 'If you hadn't started talking about God and graven images the subject would never have occurred to him.'

'I know,' said Lydia, 'but it was funny. They couldn't really disapprove of him, though they *longed to,* because he's studying for the ministry.'

'I liked the doctor,' said Betty after a while, getting on to firmer ground. 'He was a friendly little man.'

'He's got a nasty dirty little mind,' said

Lydia, 'like a puddle in a pig sty.'

'Oh *Lydia,*' said Betty, exasperatedly.

'Oh, all right,' said Lydia. 'He wasn't too bad, but he kept copying the way I said "country" in a very meaningful fashion and it got on my nerves. He says he wants me to meet some of his friends. Can you imagine why?'

'Perhaps he thinks you'd get on,' said Betty sarcastically, '–have a lot in common.'

'So likely,' said Lydia.

'Hywel was rather quiet,' said Betty.

'He hated us all being in his house,' said Lydia, 'but he put up with it quite prettily in the end. Did you see his face when he first came into the room? He looked as though we were a bunch of minks in his chicken coop.'

'A lot of men are like that,' observed Betty. 'They work hard all day. Then they just want to put their feet up.'

'Yeah,' said Lydia, but she thought there was more to it than that. Hywel's expression of blank black hostility had included her. He had wanted none of them in his house. Not even Elizabeth, she thought, remembering his look when his wife had greeted him, calmly ignoring his mood. She was playing with fire, in Lydia's opinion. Men didn't like having their moods ignored. There were two shotguns in the hall of the farmhouse. 'Ouch,' she said.

'What's wrong?' asked Betty.

'I was thinking how very unpleasant it must be to be shot.'

'Why?' asked Betty reasonably.

'It would make horrible great holes in you,' explained Lydia, 'and I imagine it would hurt like hell.'

'I mean, why were you thinking about it,' said Betty.

'I don't know,' said Lydia vaguely, 'dark passions, frustrated desires, people just being annoying. I often thought if I'd been married to Finn and I'd had a gun handy, I'd've widowed myself more than once.' It was the first time she had thought of Finn all evening.

'You ought to forget Finn,' advised Betty.

'I just did,' said Lydia.

Betty ignored this, because it was too simple and it detracted from her role of comforter. 'You must get on with your life, and think about work, and not waste all your time in regrets.'

Lydia parked the car in the overgrown lay-by. 'Do I give that impression?' she asked, switching off the ignition and wondering at the stupidity of people.

'You do a bit,' said Betty with a note of true concern, and quite taking the wind out of Lydia's sails, who wondered whether it was true that she had been seriously wounded and was repressing her hurt to the detriment of her psyche. It could be nasty, that. People were always saying so. Anxiously she probed the wound. Did she agonizingly miss the faithless Finn who had deserted her for a cross-eyed creature? Did she contain a lake of unshed, festering tears? She waited for realisation, for pain to smite her. It didn't. It was just bloody irritating.

'I'm over Finn,' Lydia announced, getting out of the car. 'I was upset for a while, but I don't seem to care any more. I expect I'm just very facile. I shall spend the rest of the hols seducing Hywel or racing round the valleys after Beuno.'

Betty, who was also getting out of the car, paused. 'You mustn't,' she said flatly.

Lydia blinked at her through the misty light of the headlamps. 'Why not?' she enquired, expecting a dissertation on the nature of people who interfered with the marriage bond.

'Because he's studying for the priesthood,' said Betty.

Oho, thought Lydia. Oho.

She was smiling all over her face as they crossed the stream, Betty nimbly discovering the stepping-stones and Lydia getting her feet wet. Lydia felt with her left hand for the keyhole, while with her right she attempted to insert the key, and then stood still. 'Do you hear it?' she asked. Her fingers had begun to tingle as though with pins and needles. It was her usual response to shock. Near misses with the car, odd noises in the night always caused her fingers to feel like this.

'What?' asked Betty.

Lydia got the door open without answering. She had lit the candles before she spoke again. She closed the door.

'What is it?' Betty looked puzzled in the candlelight. 'What's the matter?'

'There's someone laughing out there,' said Lydia. They stared at each other in silence, their roles reversed: Lydia fearful and Betty courageous.

'Let me listen,' said Betty decisively. 'I'm going to open the door and listen.'

She didn't open the door too widely and she didn't go outside, but she listened assiduously. 'I think I can hear something,' she said after a while. 'It's coming from the left.'

'It's coming from the right,' said Lydia, 'and I can hear it as clear as a bell.'

I listened to them. I stood by the open window and the dogs licked my hands as I listened.

They said, 'Elizabeth, you are wonderful to look after her the way you do', and 'Elizabeth, you are wonderful to cook as you do', and 'Elizabeth, what would Hywel have done without you?' and 'Elizabeth, what a difference you have made to the house', and 'Elizabeth, Elizabeth'.

Once I heard Hywel laugh. And Beuno talked and talked, and one by one they all laughed. But when all the people had gone no one laughed, and after a while no one spoke any more.

She had put the doll she gave me on my bed. It has yellow hair, and its eyes open and shut, and it is dead.

'I ate too much last night,' said Betty at what would have been breakfast if they'd made any. 'I shall just have a cup of camomile tea.'

Lydia made coffee and pushed the door wide open. The sun shone warm and the air was now very pure: a calm reflective day, not given to laughter.

'You didn't eat much,' said Betty.

'No,' agreed Lydia. Her imagination had suggested to her that dinner in a Welsh farmhouse might comprise mutton redolent of wild herbs, or native lobster winged from the coast by landrover. It had conjured up visions of arcane Celtic stews bubbling mysteriously in metal vessels, and bitter rowan-beer strengthened by the bodies of songbirds. But Elizabeth read women's magazines and had offered them quiche and Coronation Chicken and melon balls in wine glasses. The men had drunk canned beer and the women sweet wine. Lydia had once read a women's magazine-type romance in book-form and her mind had felt then as her stomach felt now – ever so slightly destroyed. Women's magazines had a lot to answer for, thought Lydia, with their embroidered jumpers, their mackerel and mandarin oranges, their stories of the nurse who gets the surgeon, the typist who gets the boss, contrasting so starkly with the bewildered anguish manifested by their love-ruined readers on the letters page.

There was a grey squirrel nipping up and down a hazel tree near the stream. It was neat and elegant, like all wild animals, with an air of aristocratic insouciance and good breeding. The silly sheep, the witless pheasants, the dumb cows bred by man for his own purposes had lost all joy and definition, needing to be doused, medicated, imprisoned and fed until, poor bourgeois, they were ready to be killed. Beuno came walking into Lydia's meditation. He was like the squirrel with his bright clear skin, his healthy curls and gleaming eyes: not at all a sullen, greedy, domestic beast, destined for an ignominious end.

He came at eleven o'clock, which seemed to Lydia a reasonable hour, an indication of natural good manners. Betty looked pleased to see him. Lydia found it impossible to imagine a mate for Beuno. Like the squirrel, he should marry only someone of precisely the same blood lines as himself. Anything else would be grotesquely unsuitable.

'How's Angharad?' asked Betty, who had, last night, discussed at length with Elizabeth the problems and frustrations of bringing up a defective child and felt thus freed to go on talking about it.

'I've hardly seen her,' said Beuno. 'She keeps out of my way. She keeps out of everyone's way if she possibly can.'

'Elizabeth's been trying to change that,' Betty told him, although he must surely have known already.

'Elizabeth worries too much,' said Beuno. 'There isn't anything to be done about it now. It's best to let her go her own way. Elizabeth has a townswoman's fears. Angharad is safer on the hills than she is indoors. Most days her path and Hywel's cross. He usually knows pretty well where she is.'

Lydia had just realised why Elizabeth was childless. She was afraid. She was afraid she would have a defective child because she had seen in Angharad what could happen in her husband's family. She really could not, under the circumstances, be expected to love Angharad, thought Lydia, remembering the hostility and anger which Elizabeth had so briefly exhibited last night. How could you love a child who, because of its strangeness and deformity, precluded you from having a child of your own because it might bear the same strangeness and deformity? It seemed remarkable that Elizabeth should be as good as she was to her sister-in-law. Lydia thought herself very slow not to have realised all this before, but then she reflected that the rapidity with which they had learned the circumstances of this secluded family was in itself strange. Elizabeth was lonely and Beuno guileless. Were these two qualities sufficient in themselves to cause their owners to lay all secrets bare? I suppose they must be, thought Lydia, shrugging, and wondering also whether the modern tendency, which was American in origin, to tell everybody everything before they'd even got the first olive off the cocktail stick had percolated as far as here. In the old days you kept your lunatics and your shapeless in the west wing, if you ran to one. Otherwise the attic or the coal cellar had to suffice, but concealment had been the fashion. Now, many people as they retrieved their fingers from the handshake were likely to tell that their husband had just fathered an illegitimate child and ask your advice on how to proceed, or offer to give you the telephone number of their analyst/ acupuncturist/homeopath/hypnotist who had been so helpful over their drink problem. No one hesitated to tell you that their spouse was schizophrenic, they themselves alcoholic, homosexual or beastlily promiscuous (no, they were all rather proud of that one) or, of course, that they hated their mother. It had not always been so, Lydia knew. And it was the teeniest bit boring, having largely absorbed the shock element that had once added a prurient interest to social intercourse.

'I'm going for a walk,' said Beuno, 'because Hywel wants me to help dip the sheep and I hate the things.'

'You're a shepherd of men,' said Betty, and Lydia hoped she wasn't going to be roguish.

'Do you take the view that God exists?' asked Lydia. 'Or do you see him as an inconvenient remnant of outmoded superstition – a bit like a gallstone – of which we must all be purged before religion can take on its true form, that is, without him?'

Beuno turned to look at her. 'They've all been thinking,' he said. 'I wish they wouldn't.'

'I thought it was good to think,' said Betty.

'There you are,' said Lydia. 'There's a limit to what you can think about God.'

Beuno agreed. 'It's when they think he's a gallstone they find it difficult.'

'Don't you mind being in a Church that doesn't believe in God?' asked Betty.

'It's only a few of them who don't believe,' explained Beuno. 'The academics. They get embarrassed at High Table if they think their peers imagine they do. They have to explain that although they're priests they're really not credulous nitwits, and then they feel they have to go further and they end up writing books about it and yapping away on

74

the television.' He added tranquilly: 'No one takes much notice of them.'

Lydia was pleased with him. It was seldom she met someone with whom she was in religious accord. Finn hadn't believed in anything; not even that the Ancient of Days had dwindled to a gallstone. Some of their worst rows had resulted from this incompatibility. 'I like God,' she said.

'You don't show much sign of it,' accused Betty. 'You never go to church and you're not very charitable.'

'I know,' said Lydia, 'but God makes me laugh.'

'Perhaps you make *him* laugh,' suggested Betty. 'Perhaps it's him you keep hearing.'

'That is not impossible,' said Lydia. 'But it's more likely to be the little fat chap who laughs when people make love.'

'Cupid?' asked Betty cautiously.

'No, no,' said Lydia. 'This one's much older, and oriental in appearance. He sits on a very smokey-looking cloud and he laughs and laughs at the sight of copulation. All his stomachs and his chins wobble. He has to hang on to them with his hands.'

After a moment Betty said, 'I don't know what you're talking about.'

'This god,' said Lydia. 'The one who

invented sex. He did it for a laugh.'

Betty glanced appealingly at Beuno. 'I thought you were a Christian,' she said to Lydia. 'One God.'

'I am a Christian,' said Lydia. 'This little god is the product of my imagination.'

'Then how do you know the other one isn't as well?' demanded Betty, seeing that a point might be scored here.

'I know my imagination,' said Lydia. 'I can't imagine the other one.'

'Then how do you know he's there?' asked Betty.

'I know he's there because I can't imagine him,' explained Lydia patiently. 'If I could I should be extremely doubtful. He'd resemble Santa Claus or someone. Anyone I can imagine is quite unlikely to exist.'

'We could talk about God at the same time as walking,' said Beuno. 'I'll show you the place where the convent used to be in the Middle Ages.'

'I want to walk up the other valley too,' said Betty. 'Someone told me the hedge is centuries old. According to Hooker's hypothesis.'

They went across the fields and came to a place where a few stones lay, giving no indication at all that they had once combined to form a dwelling for holy women.

'The Welsh name for the bridge over there,' said Beuno, gesturing, 'means "the place where the milk was spilt" because one year the nuns' cow went dry and they had to go down to the village to beg for some, and they got this far and then one of them dropped it.'

'And they all said, Hereinafter and for evermore let this place be known as the place where the milk was spilt,' said Betty dreamily.

'Well, I suppose when they'd finished saying bugger and blast and damn and kicking butter-fingers in the head they might get round to saying that,' said Lydia.

'Angharad used to spend a lot of time here,' said Beuno. 'There, where the leaves come down to the water. She'd hide in there for hours.'

'Who looked after her when she was little?' asked Betty, who had learned that Angharad's mother had died giving birth to her.

'Hywel mostly,' said Beuno. 'The women from the village used to come and help, but it was mostly him.'

Both Betty and Lydia found this odd and wanted to know how they'd managed.

Beuno considered, politely. 'I suppose we must have had more help than I remember,' he said after a while. 'I don't remember that she was ever much trouble. I was much younger than Hywel, so I suppose he bore the brunt of it, but I don't remember him complaining. We look after our own. We're used to it. We've been used to it for centuries. There was never anyone else to turn to here, over the hills and far away, and there's an ancient tradition of mistrusting strangers. Even Elizabeth has got it now.' He smiled at them reassuringly. 'If you stay long enough you will look with suspicion on unfamiliar faces.'

Lydia, picturing Hywel's dark eyes, thought that he'd probably have put up with a great deal rather than have strangers in his house.

'Hywel didn't like having people around,' said Beuno. 'For years before he married Elizabeth I don't think anyone came to the house except for the old men on Sunday after chapel. I didn't think he'd ever marry.'

It was an unlikely match. Lydia tried to imagine a more suitable bride for the dour Hywel and could see only a dim, faintly female version of himself. 'I suppose he got an ache in the loins,' she said.

'*Lydia,*' said Betty.

'Will you marry?' Lydia asked Beuno.

'*Lydia,*' said Betty.

'I don't think so,' said Beuno. 'I want to comb God's hair. If I married I'd only end up cleaning his shoes. You can't love God and anyone else.'

'I do so agree with you,' said Lydia, relieved. There was something most unpleasing and incongruous about the idea of Bueno shackled to a wife.

'The Church has always had trouble with marriage,' said Beuno, 'trying to combine two mutually exclusive imperatives. The vicar's wife is usually a pain. Like the doctor's wife.'

'Or the king's wife,' said Lydia, 'or the politician's wife. Appendages – being hauled round like a penitent's placard.'

'Whose wife *do* you like?' asked Betty.

'Nobody's,' said Lydia. 'Wives are a bad thing. So are husbands.'

'You'd have married Finn like a shot if he'd asked you,' said Betty, losing her temper and speaking wildly.

Lydia was sitting on a stile with the sun behind her and Beuno beside her. Betty faced them with the sun in her eyes. She could hardly see them. Lydia wasn't smiling in her usual maddening way, but Betty thought she was; and she thought perhaps Beuno was smiling too. 'Don't deny it,' she said.

'I'm not,' said Lydia, pacifically, after a while. She didn't want to make Betty cry here in a field in the summer. Her motive was only partly compassionate. It would be very disgusting if Betty were to burst into tears in the sunshine; Lydia sat still and sighed, waiting. She knew the recent conversation had been fantastical, with faint cruel undertones, and that it had excluded Betty, who was a good little thing. She now felt herself to be like the squirrel, staring with bright inimical eyes at a sad domestic beast. But if Betty began to weep Lydia would be, in humanity, bound to put her arm about her in consolation; so she said earnestly that she was suddenly terribly hungry and could it possibly be time for lunch.

'Betty is a wonderful cook,' she said, as they walked slowly back across the fields. 'And she knows all about wild mushrooms and things.' The conversation had become intensely boring.

I saw them in the field with the fallen stones. Beuno was talking. He always talks like that. I went home through the field with the cows. The cows of my country are small and black, and the cats, and the eyes of my countrymen.

80

Betty cooked lunch happily. Lydia even brought her some dandelion leaves. Beuno didn't suggest that Elizabeth would be expecting him back, but ate his omelette as casually and thoughtlessly as the squirrel who had moved off to eat nuts in a different hazel tree.

'Betty is turning into a vegetarian,' explained Lydia; 'so we lean rather heavily on the egg.' She regarded Beuno, thinking how fortunate she was to discover one of her own kind in this improbable environment.

Betty thought he looked more like a gipsy than a minister – a good gypsy. It was ridiculous to suppose that he would never marry. Even Catholic priests were getting married now. Betty detested waste.

'Why do you suppose I keep hearing laughter?' Lydia was asking idly. She had drunk several glasses of wine and didn't really care at the moment.

'I think there's something wrong with your hearing,' said Betty, in a hurry because speculation on this could easily lead to the sort of conversation that she didn't like. 'I think you should go and see the doctor.'

'OK,' said Lydia, bibulously obedient.

'You ought to go tonight,' said Betty,

'before it gets any worse. I'm going down to the shop later, so I'll make an appointment for you.'

I was in the graveyard at noonday. The shadows were sparse and the light was cruel, as though the noonday devil had taken more than his share out of malice and greed. There is a time in the day when the days are long, when the edge of light meets the edge of darkness and for a moment there is nothing.

I stood on my grave and my flesh knew all there is to know of clay, and my bones of stone. All the grasses stood still in the wicked sunlight until the evil had to loosen its hold, and the shadows came back, and a little breeze, and the earth began to turn again.

It is light which is to be feared. The darkness is nothing, and beyond it is another light, and I won't be dead. I won't be dead...

When the fumes of the wine had dissipated themselves Lydia said she wouldn't go and see the doctor. She said she hated doctors. She said they were quite untrustworthy and cut off people's arms and legs unnecessarily in order to keep their hand in, demonstrate their skills and prove that they were earning their money. The fumes of the wine had not been entirely dissipated and she felt too lazy to go all the way to the village and tell Dr Wyn about her ears. Her ears, she claimed, were perfectly sound. If she heard laughter that wasn't there it was not her ears but her brain which was at fault, and she wished to preserve her experience intact in order to present it freshly to the specialist whom she intended to consult when her holiday was over.

'If I start gassing about it to the local vet,' she said, 'it'll get all stale and distorted, and I shall be so bored with it I shan't be able to talk about it at all.'

Lydia's stubbornness would make Betty look a fool in the eyes of the doctor, so she got cross. 'You *must* go,' she said, 'I had an awful time persuading him to see you. He's fitting you in at the end of all his appointments.'

This wasn't true. The lady who fixed the appointments had said 6 o'clock without any messing about.

At 5.45 Lydia walked down the path to the car, marvelling at the power which people like Betty could wield merely by threatening to sulk. As she came to her car she met Hywel, homeward-bound on his tractor. He swung up a hand in a non-committal gesture and rumbled on. With some pique Lydia understood that he had decided against finding her interesting. Driving along the lane, she tried to picture Hywel parking his tractor and going into his house to be greeted by Elizabeth, and found it impossible. She could visualise only dimness and silence, and Hywel in a state of wrathful wonder at finding that alien woman, his wife, in his mother's house. Hywel seemed to her like some hapless creature in a story, spellbound by despair, made powerless by circumstance, trapped by a ruthless magic without even the faery consolation of glamour, the illusion of delight. For Elizabeth she felt no sympathy, since presumably no one had forced her to enter Farmhouse Grim. Hywel, supposed Lydia, must have briefly courted her, have put on a suit, taken her out to a café, been moderately gay. But even so Elizabeth should have known what she was walking into, should have looked closely at the encircling fields, the rock-built house and Hywel all muddy and iced and quiet from winter toil.

When Lydia had marvelled to Betty about the horror of Elizabeth's existence, Betty had told her not to be so silly. I'm not being so silly, thought Lydia, resentfully. That's a miserable farmhouse, and the people in it are perilously unhappy or I'm a monkey's uncle.

She was still brooding as she reached the surgery, which was situated in a superior house of dressed stone set among laurel bushes and bits of lawn. She sat in the waiting-room, which contained only one other patient – a child with ringworm, his mother in tow. She ignored the child, fearing contamination, and tried to imagine Elizabeth's wedding. Probably, she concluded, it had just washed itself along on a tide of alcohol and that uneasy mixture of salaciousness and sanctimoniousness which characterises these melancholy occasions.

She had just begun to worry about the honeymoon, finding an image of Hywel in Benidorm particularly elusive, when she was summoned by the doctor. How difficult it was, she now reflected, to speak of one's physical ailments to a person with whom one has dined. How wise was her father. She lied to Dr Wyn, saying that she had wrenched her shoulder, since although there was nothing inherently shameful about noises in the head she did not wish to confide in him. How glad I am, she thought simply, that I have not suddenly contracted syphilis.

He bade her remove her shirt, and moved her arm around, while occasionally and at random she remarked 'Ouch'.

'Not much wrong there,' he told her. 'Don't use it for a few days, and see how it goes.' He appeared to be as bored with Lydia's shoulder as she was herself. He had something else on his mind. 'I'm glad you called in this evening,' he said. 'Not in a hurry, are you? Got a few minutes?'

'Y-e-s,' said Lydia cautiously.

'Someone I want you to meet,' he announced, flinging open a door behind him and ushering Lydia into a sitting-room.

'This is April,' he said, indicating a nondescript, darkish girl who sat on a corner of the sofa. He didn't tell the girl who Lydia was; so Lydia knew her reputation had gone before her.

The girl glanced at her craftily. She wore a faintly sly and greedy look, like a child who has been promised a rather disreputable treat if it's good.

Lydia, who had quite often been subjected to this experience, twigged at once. Dr Wyn had told his friends that Lydia could be relied on to say something awful, or to sink, senseless, under the table. She was the floor show.

Dr Wyn introduced her to a tall foolish-looking man who was pouring whisky at a side table, and whose name she didn't catch.

'How do you do,' said Lydia tonelessly. She, as it were, took her personality, folded it up and sat on it.

'I think it's ever so pretty here, don't you?' she said. 'Such a change from the city. I often say to my friend I wish I could retire and live here all the time.'

'Have another drink,' offered Dr Wyn, looking rather puzzled.

'Oooh, no I mustn't,' said Lydia, who longed for one. 'I've got such a silly head. Spirits make it go round and round. Tee, hee, hee.'

I have broken Elizabeth's doll. I threw it on the cobble-stones and Elizabeth cried. I cannot speak. If I could speak, they would say I am mad. Because I cannot speak, they say I am mad. Elizabeth said to Hywel it was her doll when she was a little girl and she had loved it, and Hywel said, 'More fool you.' And she dried her eyes.

Beuno buried the doll under a rowan tree. She cried to Bueno that it had been her doll when she was a little girl and she had loved it, and he took the spade, and dug a hole, and buried it.

I thought I would dig it up again, and put it in her bed, all covered with mould, so that she would know it was dead, but after a while she stopped crying, so I left it there. I hid among the rocks and Hywel came looking for me. He couldn't find me. I waited until the shadows filled the valley before I went home.

Beuno said 'Oh Angharad' when I went upstairs, but no one else said anything.

'He wheeled me in as the star turn,' said Lydia indignantly when she got back. 'He didn't give a toss for my – ears. He just wanted to use me as a sort of social-aid-cum-aphrodisiac. I do detest social climbers. They leave muddy boot-marks on your shoulders, and you get glimpses of quite their least attractive aspects. So I sat there thinking about life, and when I listened again he was talking about orgasms.' She paused, squinting reflectively. '*Could* he've been? Yes, he was, because, after that, he started going on about nights of love. I do seem to have the most extraordinary effect on people. Or do you suppose he does it all the time?'

'I don't think he does it at all,' said Betty. 'I think it's your imagination again.'

'I don't imagine that sort of thing,' protested Lydia. 'What I just told you is straight reportage. I think I've even left out the worst bits. Blocked them. I'm beginning to think this valley is a sort of extended nut-house.'

'It's you who keep hearing things,' Betty reminded her.

'It's probably one of them,' said Lydia, '–one of the lunatics giggling away in the night.'

Both women wished that this had not been said.

Betty went over and locked the door, and Lydia looked out of the window at the shadows that were gathering under the trees. 'They don't like us, you know,' she told Betty.

'Oh, nonsense,' said Betty. 'What about Elizabeth's dinner party? If they didn't like us they wouldn't've asked us, would they?'

'It wasn't them,' said Lydia. 'Elizabeth asked us, and she isn't one of them. If it wasn't for her we'd never have set foot in Farmhouse Grim. They don't like outsiders.'

'What about Beuno?' asked Betty. 'He likes us.'

'It's his Christian duty to do so,' said Lydia. 'Beuno likes everyone a little and no one in particular. He's a true religious.'

'I have come to the conclusion,' said Betty, who had also been thinking, 'that the reason Beuno doesn't marry is the same as the reason Elizabeth won't have children. They're afraid of heredity. It's Angharad. I saw her today. Poor little girl.' She looked faintly stunned, as people do who have observed the misshapen: there is no Schadenfreude to ease the witnessing of deformity.

Lydia shivered and knelt to light the fire. The flames were pure, but then she remembered the ash in the morning. She thought of water, which was pure, and then remembered the crud on the bed of the stream. She thought that everything was composed of heat and corruption and water – that we live off death and water – and she resented her own blinding mortality. 'I know God originally intended me for an angel,' she said crossly, brushing wood shavings from her knees. 'I wonder what dreadful thing I did to end up as a human being?'

'I'm never sure you are a human being,' said Betty repressively. 'You're very peculiar.'

'That's the nicest thing you've ever said to me,' said Lydia. 'I saw the Molesworths outside their house. I'd rather be a rat than a Molesworth. I'd rather live in Farmhouse Grim than Château Molesworth. I'd rather be a rat and his wife than be April or a doctor.'

'April?' said Betty. 'The Molesworths' daughter is called April. It must've been her.'

'Oh help,' said Lydia. 'What a good thing I went all quiet. I could've said something frightful.'

'As if you cared,' said Betty.

'Oh, come on,' said Lydia. 'I do know where to draw the line.'

The day of the Agricultural Fair approached and passions rose in the village. In the shop Lydia heard rumours of men who sat up all night amongst their carrots, a shotgun across their knees for fear of jealous rivals who would come under cover of darkness to pour paraquat on the feathery fronds; of women who stood all night in their kitchens baking, baking in the quest for the one, the perfect, cake or loaf. In the hills men and women were combing and washing and polishing chosen animals to a *Vogue*-like perfection of appearance, winners determined to hold their titles, aspirants determined to displace them.

'Oo-er,' said Lydia. 'They alarm me. I begin to get some idea of what the Roman games must've been like.'

'All villages are the same,' said Betty. She had acquired a copy of the rules of the various competitions and was reading it. 'There's a section here for the most prettily arranged salad. Shall I try?'

'You wouldn't stand a cat in hell's chance,' said Lydia. 'It's all rigged beforehand.' She had now grown quite used to Betty who had, on the whole, been very patient with her; and, once accepted, it was restful having someone around to do the cooking and the washing-up. She had so far relented towards Betty that she did not wish to see her disappointed. 'We'll just go along as onlookers,' she said, 'and cheer whenever it seems appropriate. Then they won't be cross with us for interfering in their primitive rituals.'

'Do you want to go to it?' asked Betty, looking up in surprise. 'I'd have thought you'd be bored.'

'Nothing would persuade me to miss it,' said Lydia. 'I always go to tribal events, wherever I am.'

For some reason this made her think of Finn, and she stood still for a moment, again waiting cautiously for any twinges of anguish, any signs of unhealed wounds. There were none. She didn't even wish he'd break a leg. She didn't care if he broke a leg or not. She looked across the stream, through the leaves at the distant field; at the nettles and the meadow-sweet and the wild roses; down at the camomile daisies crushed under her feet.

'Very, very pretty,' she approved, aloud. She was cured. Oh, the relief.

'You're looking much better recently,' said Betty, observing this show of gladness. 'Have you quite stopped hearing things?'

'Not so much as a titter,' Lydia answered her, breathing deeply. Now she could get on with life, concern herself with the large airy matters like God and death and the problem of suffering; forget, for a while, the goblin things – sex and money and regular meals.

Beuno was standing in the stream with his back to them, not doing anything.

'What's Beuno doing?' asked Betty, mop in hand, sweating slightly from the exertion of housework, Martha to the life.

'He isn't doing anything,' said Lydia. 'He's just standing in the stream.'

'I wonder if he'd run me to the shop,' said Betty. She had asked Elizabeth and Dr Wyn to come in for a drink that evening. She had wanted to ask the Molesworths too, but

Lydia wouldn't let her. 'There are some people,' Lydia had said, 'who, as it were, belong in my house, and there are some that I can tolerate. And then there are those than whom I would rather have mice, and into this latter category fall the Molesworths.' She had not spoken so elaborately for some time, and Betty knew the warning signs; so, whereas with anyone else she would have appealed to their better nature, in this case she held her tongue.

'I'm going to make some cheese straws,' she said, 'and maybe fry some onion rings. I'd get some sausages, but I don't know what's in them.'

'Pure pig,' said Lydia. 'That's pig lips, pig toenails, pig...'

'Oh, shut up,' said Betty.

Beuno said, 'There's a funeral in the church tomorrow.'

'Someone must have died,' said Lydia. She had wakened in the night with the fear of death upon her and was presently inclined to a harsh and flippant approach to the subject.

'That is usually the case when a funeral is planned,' said Beuno.

Yes,' said Lydia, 'a funeral would feel pointless without a body. I like funerals.

They're so much more satisfactorily final and distinguished than weddings; and christenings always fill me with great unease and pessimism and I don't like sugared almonds.'

'I think weddings are the worst,' said Beuno. 'There's always someone with their fingers crossed. I think it's usually the mother of the groom. What will I do when I have to officiate at one? I shall have to have a long talk with the Lord beforehand.'

'And the bride and groom,' said Lydia. 'You'll have to invite them into the vicarage and try and dissuade them, and then when they're stubborn you'll have to elaborate on the Christian concept of matrimony.'

'The Lord will provide,' said Beuno. 'Did I tell you how people die in this valley?' he asked.

'Do they have a special mode?' asked Lydia.

'They put clean nightdresses on, and they straighten their bed, and then they lie down with their hands crossed on their chest. I see it like this. The Angel of Death looks in and he says: "You've got five minutes to get your clean nightdress on, and arrange your effects, and put the cat out, and tear up that compromising letter, and then I'll be back for you." And instead of arguing about it – they do.'

'I wonder if I would?' mused Lydia. 'Or would I start screaming that I'd left a soufflé in the oven, or forgotten to get the coat back from the cleaners, or I was too young to die...'

'Die?' asked Dr Wyn with professional interest, manoeuvring himself and April over the stepping-stones.

'Hi,' said Lydia. 'Go on up to the cottage while I get my shoes on.' She whispered to Beuno that they must both be very boring now, very staid, because she utterly refused to amuse Dr Wyn. She thought that it was odd that she should be so certain of Beuno's allegiance with her against one of his countrymen, but she had no doubts of him. 'I didn't know April was coming,' she said. 'I don't think we asked her.'

'He'll drag her round everywhere for a time,' said Beuno, 'and then he'll get sick of her, or find some other girl who takes his fancy. He's been doing it for years. You may not have noticed, but there's an awful lot of bachelors in the valley. Their mothers tell them no one is good enough for them. It happens in rural communities.'

Lydia watched Betty ushering the guests

into the cottage. 'If you see me drinking too much,' she said to Beuno, 'you must tie up my throat like a cormorant, or I shall start speaking wildly.'

'Wyn disapproves of me,' said Beuno. 'He thinks the ministry is an affectation and a waste of time, and on the other hand he thinks priests should be very good, and he doesn't think I am because he's known me for so long, so he's annoyed with me. He'll probably take no notice of you because he'll be trying to upset me.'

'It sounds like another wonderful evening,' said Lydia. 'I wonder where Elizabeth is.'

'She's been looking after Angharad,' said Beuno. 'It always takes her some time to get ready. She'll be along later.' He spoke noncommittally, and Lydia understood that there were things of which Beuno would not yet speak to her. She didn't mind. There was no point in being curious about hopeless situations.

'We'll be there,' Dr Wyn was saying, as they entered the kitchen. 'Won't we, darling?'

'Yes,' said April, making it increasingly apparent that she was a girl of very few words.

'She's doing a flower arrangement for the competition. What is it this year, darling?

Three dahlias, a book-end and a brass orna-
ment?'

Lydia imagined this to be a joke and was
surprised when April concurred. She glanced
at her for signs of irony and saw none.

'Her mum always wins the malt-loaf section,' claimed the doctor with vicarious
pride.

Lydia thought moodily that she couldn't
hope to be as boring as Dr Wyn if she tried
all night. Nevertheless she made an attempt.
'How many sections are there?' she enquired.

This was a mistake, because the doctor
told her.

By the time Elizabeth arrived Lydia was
prepared to welcome her, since any ad-
ditional flavour must add something to the
evening, which was like Betty's meatless
stock into which she kept putting more and
more dried herbs and burned onion in an
effort to make it taste of something. It was
the sort of evening on which Lydia would
normally get drunk and move into a world of
her own, highlighted by strange insights,
hectically and artificially tuppence-coloured.
Grimly, she quaffed lemon squash.

Elizabeth told Betty that Wyn had been to
school with Hywel, and Betty told Elizabeth

that she had heard that the Welsh standard of education was very high.

Sip, went Lydia at her lemon squash.

Betty deplored the cuts in the education budget and Beuno lit a cigarette.

'Smoking?' queried the doctor. 'Giving us all pneumoconiosis?' He fixed Lydia with a meaning glance. 'Guess where I'm going this weekend,' he invited her. Sensibly he did not wait for a reply, since the possibilities were clearly endless. 'London,' he told her, staring at her with an air of triumph.

Well, I don't care, thought Lydia I hope it stays fine for you. She was puzzled by the doctor's manner. He spoke as children speak. I've got something you haven't got was his meaning.

Elizabeth got up suddenly, walked to the window and looked out. After a moment she sat down again. She didn't speak.

'Can I get you anything?' asked Betty.

'Nothing,' said Elizabeth, 'thank you.' For no apparent reason she uttered a little laugh.

'I live in London,' ventured Lydia.

'Yes, I know,' said the doctor, still staring at her. So that wasn't it.

'I'm here on holiday,' Lydia explained further.

'I know,' said the doctor.

Lydia sipped her squash, thinking. Her original conclusion was correct. The doctor was telling her that he was off to have a good time where Lydia lived, imagining that this would induce envy in her. She stared thoughtfully into her lemon squash. The trouble with people like Dr Wyn was that there was really no answer to the jaw-dropping remarks they made. She could hardly observe aloud that the subject of his weekend was very boring.

'You'll find it pretty tedious at the moment,' she said. 'There's absolutely no one there but tourists swarming all over the place.' Another component of the doctor's teasing was, she suspected, an acute resentment of her supposedly exalted position in the world of journalism. 'It's hell just at present. Like a bottle you expect to have whisky in and it turns out to be full of a specimen for the doctor.' She beamed at him over the rim of her glass.

'You know you get bored here too, Lydia,' Betty reminded her.

'Yes, I know,' conceded Lydia, 'but then I dash off somewhere else to see something different.' She wondered whether the doctor imagined that because she was here without a man she hadn't got one. She shrank from his crudity and his playground teasing. There was something clumsily sadistic in teasing: signs of an almost homicidal inadequacy and despair. Lydia wondered whether he was impotent. His insistence on sexual matters could not be merely attributable to his calling, since not all doctors carried on like that. Perhaps it was caused by the complicated influences of the valley where the men seemed so often to remain unmarried, sometimes perhaps because, as Beuno held, their mothers said there was no one good enough for them, sometimes because there simply wasn't anyone. And there was the residue of a chapel-rooted misogyny quite usual in remote rural communities. It was dispiriting and chilling, and the teasing was its outward and visible form. These men jeered and poked sticks through the bars at creatures they secretly, at once, feared and desired.

Elizabeth stood up again. 'I must go back to Angharad,' she said.

'Don't go,' said the doctor, lying back in his chair and smiling at her lazily.

Lydia was furious. How dare he dissuade *her* guests from leaving. He was as bad as Betty. Am I so negligible, she asked herself indignantly, that everyone feels this compulsion to speak for me?

'Of course she must go,' she said, 'if she's worried about Angharad.'

'Yes,' said Elizabeth, 'I must go,' and she went.

The doctor's smile broadened.

Lydia felt oppressed and vaguely threatened.

'There's no one of any consequence in London at the moment,' she told him, 'but you won't be able to move for the millions of nobodies going to look at the Tower.'

'Oh, I'll find something to do,' he said with an air of practised lewdness.

April, who until now had been just sitting there, at this point, to give her her due, showed symptoms of unease. 'Oh, Wyn,' she said.

Lydia felt briefly sorry for her and attempted to engage her in conversation, but it was no good. She turned to Beuno and spoke of lighter matters until darkness descended.

'I thought that was a very pleasant evening,' said Betty. 'Beuno helped me with the washing-up after you went to bed.'

'I don't like Dr Wyn,' said Lydia. 'I increasingly don't like him.'

'He's a good doctor,' said Betty. 'They all say he's very good. Elizabeth says he's wonderful with Angharad. He'll go and see her any time of the day or night. Elizabeth only has to phone him.'

'He still gives me the creeps,' said Lydia.

'He's only teasing,' said Betty. 'I don't know where we should be without people like him.'

But Lydia, remembering the look on his face, thanked Heaven that she was not a child under his interested regard. 'I think he's a disappointed man,' she said. 'He's getting on and he hasn't got far. Stuck in his village forever.'

'He could've left if he'd wanted to,' said Betty. 'He's been offered all sorts of consultancies at lots of London hospitals.'

'Who said so?' demanded Lydia.

'He did,' said Betty.

'Oh, him,' said Lydia.

She knew that he had tried to give her the impression that he was going off on a promiscuous adventure and expected this to arouse in her both admiration and jealousy, but as Lydia's misdemeanours were more of the spirit than of the flesh she found promiscuity not merely sinful but foolish and disgusting.

'He is far too old to be carrying on like that,' she said censoriously. 'This obsession with sex is a sign of retardation. People who leap from one relationship to another like someone crossing a stream on stepping-stones never grow up. They are like people at a meal who can only take a bite from each course. Highly unnutritious.'

Betty said nothing because, Lydia knew, Lydia's forays into morality left her speechless.

They stayed discreetly close to the cottage as the funeral proceeded in the adjacent churchyard. Beuno had told them that funerals were known as either private or public. The private ones, being exclusive, aroused bad feelings, but to the public ones people came from miles around and were given things to eat: distant relations, old friends, old acquaintances, old enemies, but no outsiders, no aliens. Unlike the Agricultural Fair, funerals made no provisions at all for visitors. The deceased was over ninety; so Lydia and Betty had not been called upon to express great regret or commiseration among the villagers. The year Lydia had bought her cottage a young person had died and Lydia had been lost for words, as people are in the face of tragedy. All that remains to be said is incised on stone, and the living go around silently with long faces and glances that mean 'I can't tell you how sorry I am, but I do know how you feel.' And sometimes they do and sometimes they don't. Either way it is of little use to the bereft locked full of raw grief, which might one day mature into something more bearable, and might not. The bereft, at that time, have no way of knowing.

As the mourners left, Lydia heard a low laugh and sat up on her rug, thinking suspiciously of her ears. But someone real had laughed. People did laugh at funerals. The joke went on after all.

'I sometimes think it's amazing that anyone ever laughs at anything,' said Lydia when the cortege had gone away down the lane. 'When you think of everything, it really isn't funny.'

'I had an uncle who was dying of emphysema,' said Betty, 'and he used to implore people not to make him laugh because it took his breath away, and I could never understand what he could find to amuse him.'

'There you are then,' said Lydia, who had now been forced on several occasions to concede that Betty was not unsympathetic and understood more than Lydia would have thought her capable of. This was humbling, and good for Lydia's character, which stood in need of improvement. She wondered whether she heard unreal laughter as a self-inflicted punishment because she was incontinently fond of amusement and only liked people who made her laugh, no matter what their other qualities.

The gravedigger was hurling earth into the pit. They could hear him. It seemed slightly indecent to listen. Lydia felt the need to remove herself, as people who stay in hotels get out of the way when the poor chambermaids come to make the beds. She felt she should offer to help, while knowing her help was not called for.

They waited until the lane must surely be empty of funeral guests and then went down to the car. The little trees in the hedges on each side of the path reached out to each other across it like the opposing factions at a wedding: the families of the bride and groom which will never be united but must maintain a truce, unnaturally bound by the exigent complicity of the couple.

'Christenings and weddings and funerals are to life what breakfast and lunch and dinner are to the day,' said Lydia. 'None of them are strictly necessary, but they do break up all that time and give people the feeling they're doing something – achieving something. I'd just as soon make do with a packed lunch. A little viaticum.'

She felt an old resentment at being forced into a structure. There was only one way into life, one way through, and one way out, and it made Lydia mad. She had never belonged to anything and would have been a hopeless soldier. Nevertheless she was subject, with all her kind, to the overall rules: chiefly to that most irritating of all which maintains 'You shall not know, you shall not wholly understand why it is this way. You shall just get on with it.'

'Grrrr,' said Lydia, flinging back an importunate branch.

There were no locals in the pub. It had been taken over by a new contingent of tourists.

'I wonder where everyone is?' said Betty.

'Everyone seems to be here,' said Lydia. 'I mean *everyone*. I can hardly get to the bar.'

'No, I mean the locals,' said Betty. 'I don't recognise a soul.'

'They've all gone to the funeral,' said Lydia.

The locals were like a shoal of fish, gone, without exception, to another part of the water – or a flock of birds, called by some mystery to a different stretch of air.

'They'll be back,' said Lydia. She struggled to the bar and ordered a pint and a half of lager. The half was for Betty. She would want another half later, but she didn't like being faced with a full pint all at once.

The tourists were milling about, carrying brimming glasses, and beginning to boast, as they found seats, of sporting successes. Their women, already seated, were not speaking. It was for these women that Mrs Molesworth kept her gift shop. They would hang around all day, bored stiff, while the menfolk sported, would provide the statutory feminine presence in the evenings – be brought on, as it were, as the dancing girls – and as a reward would be permitted to waste money on the sheepskin rugs, the (fairly) local pottery and all the other objects of tourism that Mrs Molesworth purveyed.

It became clear from their phrases that this was a boating group come to sail about on the nearby natural lake.

Lydia and Betty pushed their way out on to the road and sat on the wall that protected the customers from passing cars. Lydia explained how much she disliked tourists.

After a while Betty protested. 'They're only people on their holiday,' she said; 'they're just enjoying themselves.'

'They couldn't enjoy *themselves*,' said Lydia. 'Are they like this at home, or is it only when they're on holiday?'

'You shouldn't hate people so much,' said Betty.

'I know,' said Lydia, 'but I can't help it.'

'Just ignore them,' said Betty.

'I would if I could,' said Lydia, 'but the thing is I wish they'd all crash their cars and die.'

Poor Lydia was truly distressed. Already a bridge at the head of the village where the local youths had been wont to gather to throw coke cans in the stream had been demolished in the interests of a road-widening development designed to encourage yet more dinghy-topped cars into the vicinity.

From where she sat she could see the Molesworth house. It stood in front of an old grey cottage which the Molesworths had bought in order to acquire the land whereon they could erect their dream home. The dream home stood and shrieked like a blatant brassy mistress proclaiming her supremacy over the poor old lovely wife, left to slow decay.

'Maybe it'll get burned down,' said Lydia hopefully.

'Don't be wicked,' said Betty. 'You're only a tourist yourself, after all. You don't belong here any more than they do.'

'My forebears came from this valley,' said Lydia.

'You never told me that before,' said Betty suspiciously. 'Is it true?'

But Lydia was drinking great mouthfuls of beer and wouldn't tell her.

They buried the old man. They opened the earth for him and they put him inside. Not too far down, because one day, the last day, he will come back again into the air. That day the bones of the brother of my mother who went to the bottom of the sea will rise up through the green waters, and when they meet the air they will take on his flesh again, and he will swim far up into the endless air and he will meet the old man, free of his dust walking in the air, and my mother flying, and me flying, and I will be laughing.

Someone laughed in the graveyard because he was an old, old man who died and no one weeps much for the old. Once I saw a woman there full of grief. She was too small for all that grief. I could see it running in her until it overflowed, and as fast as it ran more grief took its place until the lane and the streams ran with grief and all the valley was the colour of grief. She was grieving for her child. Who will grieve for me? What colour will the valley be when I die? The colour of Angharad, for I am dead.

Hywel and Beuno have gone to the funeral.

Elizabeth said, 'I will not go. I did not know him. I cannot leave Angharad alone.'When they had gone she went to the phone and she said, 'I must see you. I have to see you. I don't care.'

And when he came he was angry and he said, 'What do you want, Elizabeth? Do you want me to be struck off? For God's sake you know what they're like in the village. They'll see my car coming here and they know no one's ill and you know what they'll think.'

And she said, 'I know what they'll think and they will be quite right.'

And he said, 'Not any longer.'

And her face broke and she said, 'Oh Wyn, oh Wyn,' and he held her in his arms, and from where I crouched in the elbow of the stairs I saw his face and it was the face of the fox that Hywel killed, and the face of the stoat that he beat with a stick in the hen-yard, and the face of the dog that savaged the ewes.

Her face was below his face and she said, 'I'll say Angharad was ill again.'

He said, 'Where is Angharad?' And he lifted

111

his head and his eyes saw my eyes and he smiled.

She said, 'She's out on the hills, or down in the fields.'

And he said, 'That's good.' And his face was the face of the hawk as it stoops, and the face of the shrew as the hawk stoops.

Satan, who finds work for idle hands to do, also fills idle minds with fruitless speculation. Lydia was wondering why Elizabeth hadn't asked April to her dinner party, and also why she had been so silent on the previous evening and had left so early.

'I bet I was right first time,' she said to Betty. 'I bet he made a pass at her.'

'Who?' asked Betty, squinting in the sunlight.

'The priapic practitioner,' said Lydia, who had just thought of this appellation. 'I bet he made a pass at Elizabeth. He seems to go for plain, quiet women.'

Betty was really shocked. 'You can't go around saying things like that,' she protested. 'You'll get into terrible trouble.'

'I'm not going around saying it,' said Lydia, 'I just wondered, and I said it to you, so if it gets around it'll be you who did it.'

'As if I would,' said Betty. 'Why do you

think so?' she asked after a while, as her initial disapproval was superseded by curiosity.

'I have a feeling,' said Lydia, 'and my feelings are not to be lightly disregarded.'

'You must have some evidence,' said Betty.

'I have,' said Lydia. 'The evidence of my sixth sense. Hanky-panky, it says.'

'No,' said Betty. 'I don't believe it. He wouldn't be so stupid.'

'When you've lived as long as me,' said Lydia, speaking like the crone she would one day doubtless turn into, 'you'll know just how stupid people can be.'

Betty sat there thinking. 'If it is the case,' she said, 'I'm very sorry for Elizabeth. Hywel is a bit grumpy, and Wyn's so cheerful. She must be awfully unhappy now he's taken up with April. Then on the other hand she's got Hywel and the farm they're quite well off, you know. And she must have loved Hywel, or she wouldn't have married him.'

Lydia ignored this last asinine remark. 'They're all rather sad people,' she said, 'and they must be getting under my skin, because I quite mind about them.'

'Do you?' asked Betty.

Lydia made an instant disclaimer. 'No, of course I don't,' she said. 'What vegetarian delight is in store for supper?'

As Betty grated and chopped, Lydia wondered whether Sid and Lil knew that their daughter's suitor had laid lewd hands on the daughter of their oldest friends. Yes, of course they did. But it would not be appropriate to admit it. It was the weakness of humanity that it should disguise as strength – as sense and discretion and neighbourly feeling – an inability to recognise the more deplorable aspects of behaviour. Nice people didn't think about such things, which was why child-abuse and wife-beating went frequently unremarked.

Beuno arrived with the lengthening shadows, bearing a dead pheasant. 'I think it must've been hit by a car,' he said. 'Do you want it? Hywel won't eat it.'

Betty regarded it with a rich mixture of pity, admiration, mistrust and disgust. 'Poor thing,' she said. 'It was so beautiful. How do you know a car killed it? It might have died of disease'

Beuno swung it up to eye-level. 'It doesn't show much sign of injury,' he said, 'but as it was on the side of the road I think it's safe to assume it's just one more traffic casualty.'

Lydia took it from him. 'It doesn't look ill to me,' she said, 'apart from being dead. Its feathers look remarkably healthy.' She jiggled it up and down. 'Nice and heavy for the time of year.'

'Don't think I'm going to pluck it and cook it,' said Betty. 'If you're going to eat it you'll have to do it all yourself.'

Lydia had not imagined or expected that Betty would touch the pheasant. 'I shall hang it in the kitchen for a week,' she said, 'and then you can go out for the evening and I will have bread sauce and fried bread-crumbs, and game chips and red currant jelly and watercress and pheasant.' At the final word she swung the bird towards Betty who screamed a little.

'If you hang it in the kitchen,' Betty said, 'the gamekeeper might pass and look in and then you'll be in trouble.'

'I'll hang it in a paper bag,' said Lydia, 'and if anyone asks I'll say it's a fetish.'

'I think you should just bury it,' said Betty, and Lydia did see what she meant, for human death was attended with such ritual and dispatch that for an instant it seemed cruelly perverse to deny something similar to this helpless creature.

'If you like I'll bury his bones,' she said. 'After I've boiled them for stock of course.'

'Poor thing,' said Betty.

'People turn to vegetarianism when the

spirit fails,' said Beuno, not to anyone in particular. Nevertheless Betty looked hurt.

'They are in search of purity, perfection,' he continued, '– the perfection of the body – while within the spirit rots and withers from neglect, and without the threat of doom trembles on the edge of possibility. Exercised, massaged, bathed and pampered, carefully fed as a prize marrow, the body is an empty shell flaunted in the face of catastrophe.'

'Practising sermons?' enquired Lydia.

'Yes, I am,' said Beuno. 'What do you think?'

'Not bad,' said Lydia. 'A touch over-elaborate perhaps. The merest hint of hyperbole. What you mean to say is – everyone's scared of cancer and/or the bomb, so they put their heads in the sand and take up jogging and unrefined bran... That would be awfully difficult to do,' she said. 'I think you put it rather better yourself.'

'The body without spirit is nothing but a carcase,' continued Beuno, 'a processor for food, stamped with mortality, instinct with corruption...'

'Yes, but it is anyway,' objected Lydia, 'even when the spirit's living in it. It's still all those things you said.'

'True,' said Beuno. 'How about this...'

'You might get rather good at it,' said Lydia when he had finished declaiming in his beautiful Welsh voice. 'You might revive the revivalist tradition and galvanise the tourist trade. People might come to hear you from all over the world. How awful.'

'I don't think people want to be shouted at,' said Betty. 'I think they want to hear something encouraging and uplifting.'

'There isn't all that much on the bright side. Not if we're truthful,' said Beuno. 'Our only hope rests on the off-chance that God does exist.'

'You could say *that*,' suggested Lydia.

Beuno shrugged. 'Whatever I say,' he said, 'will probably be addressed to two old ladies and a stray sheep. All the churches are closing, as the cinemas did.'

'You mustn't be downcast,' said Lydia. 'You have a splendid opportunity to do something different and original. You can feed the hungry and comfort the oppressed and visit the sick and bury the dead. And give good counsel, and do it all with *feeling*, and people will be so amazed they'll positively flock to you. Now, as most of the country's vicars are mad, and waste all their time falling dementedly in love with middle-aged lady parishioners – whatever happened to choirboys, by the way? Oh, never mind. As I was saying, none of them do anything constructive and that's probably why they're all going mad. And all the bishops do is deny the existence of God and fool about trying to settle strikes and infuriate absolutely everyone.' On conclusion Lydia found her speech distressingly girlish and assumed a severe expression. 'Now you have the chance to revitalise the spirits of the faithful. You could have a lovely time bouncing up and down in the pulpit, screaming hell fire.'

'So could you,' Betty reminded her. 'You could go into the Church and fight for the ordination of women.'

'It wouldn't be the same,' said Lydia. 'A woman talking about hell fire would just sound like a fishwife. The priesthood needs men. There's little enough they're good for else. I think they should be left to get on with it. Women can be mothers, and men can be priests. I think that's fair. A lot of men are distraught at not being able to give birth and there's little to be done about that. It's ungrateful to want to be both.'

Betty, like many women and unlike most men, was easily swayed by argument. She immediately saw the sense in these remarks and abandoned for ever (or at least for the time being) the view that the reluctance of the Church to ordain women revealed it as bigoted and unfair. 'I wonder why everyone doesn't see that,' she remarked.

'People can be very unreasonable,' explained Beuno. 'Try and think for a moment how many points of view there are in the world and how seldom people really understand each other. There are those who practise ritual cannibalism and those like yourself who won't eat pheasants.'

'I don't understand why people want to climb mountains,' said Lydia.

'And I don't really understand the tenets of Islam,' said Beuno.

'I simply can't see how people can eat tripe,' said Betty, shuddering.

'No, I can't see that either,' agreed Lydia.

They sat for a moment in glum accord watching the evening thicken outside.

Lydia began to feel the need to laugh and reached for the vodka bottle.

'I can't really see what men see in women,' she confessed after a while. 'I sometimes think we're quite adorable, and sometimes I wonder why men get that look in their eye. I find myself looking over my shoulder to see what it is they're looking at that way. I think I'm very nice, but even on my best days I never look at myself like that. It makes me feel insecure – not understanding what it is they want so much. I don't think I've got it to offer.'

'Oh *Lydia,*' said Betty, 'of course you know.'

She glanced at Beuno for confirmation, but he looked unmoved. Clean in the lamplight, but unmoved.

'Come on,' said Betty, 'what do men see in women?'

'I don't know,' said Beuno.

Listen. Brr, brr. He isn't answering. She hangs up and starts again. He answers. She says, 'Oh, Wyn, Wyn, I can't bear it. Oh, help me please. Oh Wyn, oh Wyn... Why did you go to London? I missed you so. Oh Wyn...'

'Elizabeth looks pale,' said Betty. 'She looks tired out. I think Angharad is too much for her. She doesn't complain, but you can see she feels the tension.'

'Poor her,' said Lydia, but as she could not imagine taking care of a disruptive child she couldn't truly sympathise. She thought that Elizabeth was foolish to have married a silent countryman and to have condemned herself to a life of boredom, and that she should have known better.

'Elizabeth always takes Angharad to the Agricultural Fair for a treat. She really does her best for that girl,' said Betty.

Lydia had to admit that Betty's eagerness to admire and approve of people, while annoying, was a good characteristic and one that she herself lacked. She didn't find anyone very admirable, had reservations about people who devoted their lives to the care of the sick, and she didn't go 'Aah' over babies and brides or the Princess of Wales. She wondered whether Angharad enjoyed her treat. Lydia didn't like going out unless she was looking her best. She wondered how Angharad felt when she caught sight of her reflection in shop windows. A glimpse of herself with her hair all wrong or her coat bunched could ruin Lydia's day.

'I wonder what I should wear?' she said. 'Something smart and simple.'

'I can't see that it matters,' said Betty, 'not at the Agricultural Fair.'

'Of course it matters,' said Lydia.

'Well, I'm just going to be comfortable,' said Betty.

'So am I,' said Lydia. 'If I don't look smart

I shan't be comfortable. I shall be cross and unhappy.'

It was still early. The morning had a soft babylike tenderness upon which the post-man suddenly intruded with a postcard.

Lydia looked at the picture before she looked at the signature. It showed some women in a northern English town at the turn of the century; they were standing under an advertisement for Mazawattee tea and seemed depressed, 'Who on earth is this from?' she asked.

'If you read it you'll see,' said Betty.

'I know that,' said Lydia, 'but speculation is so interesting.'

She got a surprise when she turned it over. It was from Finn.

'Ooh,' said Lydia, enraged, 'it's from the duck. The duck is precisely the sort of person who buys second-hand postcards and carries them round and sends them to people. Left to himself, Finn would send coloured pictures of Greek beaches. He has his faults, but sepia-tinted postcards isn't one of them.'

'What does it say?' asked Betty.

'I can't read it,' said Lydia. 'I can never understand a word Finn writes.'

She had always known that Finn would reappear, because for a time they always did, never quite sure that the new woman was an improvement on the old one, keeping their options open.

'There's an exclamation mark here,' said Lydia. 'How disgusting. He must have made a little joke. There's something horribly ingratiating about exclamation marks. If he thinks he's going to get round me with his punctuation he can think again. Pah.'

'Let me see if I can read it,' said Betty. She looked at it carefully. 'They've franked over half of it,' she said. 'There's a word here that could be "lovely" and could be "lonely".'

'That's quite crucial,' said Lydia. 'It could change the meaning entirely.'

She was pleased. It is humiliating to be left and gratifying when the leaver shows signs of repentance and regret. She put the card on the dresser shelf, knowing that later she would attempt to decipher it.

'I expect he'll turn up when he gets back,' prophesied Betty.

'I expect he will,' agreed Lydia. 'I shall tell him to piss off.'

'You are hard,' sighed Betty. 'So strong.'

Lydia, however, knew that it was not strength, but vulnerability and timorousness, which led to the formation of a carapace. She did not say this to Betty, but smiled with false self-satisfaction. If Finn thought he was going to play hell with her heart he was very much mistaken, and if her carefulness made her life less rich, then that was entirely her own lookout and preferable to the interesting anguish of the uncertain love affair.

Betty was beginning to pine and to yearn after Beuno. Not too badly as yet, but the indications were there: bright eyes and heightened vivacity when he arrived, and a mild but spun-out dreariness when he went. She contrived to sit near to him and she gave him nice things to eat. Lydia told herself it was very sad, because Betty would make a wonderful vicar's wife. On the other hand she was totally out of Beuno's class. His quality of ruthless innocence rendered him unsuitable for most human intercourse. While neither a saint nor a psychopath, he clearly had some of the characteristics of both – chiefly what Lydia could only think of as a sort of selfless solipsism. He was a person of disinterested good will and he wanted no return from humankind. These people are fortunately few and far between because they are extremely odd and have a way of upsetting applecarts. Lydia could quite see Beuno maddeningly getting himself martyred on some trivial point of principle, or overturning a regime with his angelic intransigeance. If he were not so attractive she thought that she herself might, by now, have shaken him soundly.

'Beuno should be labelled "Not for human consumption",' she said, eating bread and jam. 'They are a very strange family. Each one of them is in some way cut off from the rest of society: Hywel because he's a miserable sod, Angharad because something went awfully wrong, and Beuno because he's fallen in love with God.'

'But Beuno's *normal*,' protested Betty earnestly.

Lydia spoke carefully because she did not wish to give the impression that she was attempting to divert Betty from Beuno for nefarious reasons of her own. 'I'm not saying he's raving mad,' she said, 'but he isn't like the rest of us.'

Generously, if inaccurately, she ranged herself more with Betty than with Beuno. He and she were similar but he had a natural goodness which she lacked, and she did not want to claim aloud that she understood him because that, in itself, would lead to misunderstanding.

'Finn is a fiend,' she said, 'but he's quite easy to cope with once you've accepted that. Beuno would drive one crazy.' She tried to think of the simplest way of conveying this. 'You might cook him a wonderful pie and then you'd find he'd given it to a drunken beggar, and no matter how kind you thought him after a while you'd want to kill him. Whereas Finn would never do anything like that. He'd much more likely kick a drunken beggar, but that's what most people are like and you can put up with it. Beuno is not, in everyday terms, a reasonable person.'

Betty turned the radio on, perhaps not wishing to listen to any further descriptions of Beuno's character. The radio emitted a song which Lydia associated with Finn. For a moment she was bewildered, as the real Finn and the dream Finn co-existed. The music immediately evoked the sensations, the enchantment, of being sillily in love, and simultaneously she was no longer in love. So why was she grinning like that? She was like a cured alcoholic who finds he can take a drink without again becoming addicted. It was peculiar but pleasant that she should find the song painless. A few weeks ago it would have scored claw marks on her heart.

'Ooh,' said Lydia, her hands at her breast.

'Now what?' asked Betty.

'Wouldn't it be awful if a cat scratched your heart?'

'Oh *Lydia,*' said Betty, 'you do think of the weirdest things.' She reached towards the radio.

'Don't turn it off,' implored Lydia; 'that is my favourite song.' She felt positively triumphant now. It was wonderful to be able to listen to her favourite song with impunity, extraordinary that it should still have the power to move her, but not to tears.

'You're right,' she said as she realised this could mean only one thing. 'Finn's on his way back.' She realised that at some level she had always known this, since otherwise she could not have recovered so quickly. It is noticeably more difficult to get over someone who no longer loves you than over someone who still does really.

'You must only have been infatuated with him if you've got over him so quickly,' remarked Betty repressively.

This is a distinction that agony aunts commonly make, and is of doubtful validity.

'All falling in love is infatuation,' said Lydia. 'Then if he marries you they say it's love. Then when you divorce him they say it's a tragedy because love has failed, when really it's all due to an eventual recovery from infatuation, which is a sort of brain disease.'

Besides, she thought, if Finn came back and she found him not repellent he would have been rendered kinder by his infidelity. It is only the virtuous who can be truly cruel. Guilt and a sense of common humanity make people less harsh. It was the utterly excellent Yahweh who told the malefactors to go to hell. Satan welcomed them.

Lydia shifted uneasily in her chair. It was strange how good and bad could run into each other, could appear as interchangeable: not the good of succouring the sick, nor the bad of shooting the helpless, but in the subtler regions of morality where things blended together and seemed to make the business of living easier.

'Goodness is very aggressive,' muttered Lydia into her coffee cup. It was plainly much easier to join the legions of the wicked who weren't fussy and were rather more eager for recruits than the exclusive godfearing. Satan ran the sort of club which anyone could join. Realising this, Lydia decided that she would have to aspire to the other. This conclusion made her bad tempered, since being good necessitated much thought and hard work, whereas any fool could be bad. Thinking of badness gave her one of her ideas. 'You know how the mental hospitals send people's lunatics home to them now – even the ones who think they're Napoleon or a poached egg. It's because they can't afford to keep them in, but they say it's the latest therapy technique. Well, what if the prisons did the same? The government could issue each family with a cage for their own felon, and depending on how they felt about him they'd treat him accordingly. If he was normally quite a kind person who'd taken up robbing banks because he was short of cash they could put jam on his bread and vodka in his water, and if he was a horror they could empty the potato peelings over him whenever they felt like it.'

'I never heard anything so ridiculous in my life,' said Betty.

'Self-sufficiency,' said Lydia. 'Free enterprise. Personal responsibility. Maybe you're right.' She spiked the idea, together with many others.

I am hiding. I am in the graveyard where nothing lives but the slowworm; motionless on the short grass by the path, and the little birds who search among the yews like Elizabeth in the wardrobe. She is looking for a dress for me and she is waiting to comb my hair, and she has the look on her face that she has when she guts the chickens. I will not go to the Fair. I shall hide until nightfall and eat the raspberries that grow by the stream. Hywel will go to the Fair with the cleverest dogs, but Elizabeth will not go. She will cry and say that she cannot leave the house with Angharad out on the hills alone, for anything might happen to her, anything. And Hywel will go without a word, and when he is gone and the house is silent Elizabeth will creep to the telephone and she will pick it up and it will ring in another empty house because Dr Wyn has gone to the Fair. They have the Fair in a great field where the sun beats down and the people look at me, and they see me very clearly, and they look away, and some of the children laugh and some of them cry, but they are all afraid. I would like to take each tent by the corner and pull it down, and I would untether all the neat horses and the sleek, brushed bulls and send them with a huge cry into all the hills. And the dogs would run, wailing, with their tails between their legs, and the people flee like frightened sheep, leaving Angharad, the dead, alone in a ruined field, laughing, laughing, laughing...

'It's as hot as hell,' said Lydia. 'I wish I

hadn't come. I want to go home.'

'Don't be tiresome,' said Betty. 'We've hardly seen anything yet.'

'I've seen a lot of dogs and sheep and pigs and things,' said Lydia, 'and a lot of cakes and carrots and scarlet runner-beans, and millions of people, and I want to go home.'

'It was you who wanted to come,' said Betty, irritated. 'You said you wouldn't miss it for anything.'

'I haven't missed it. I've seen it, and now I'm getting hot and cross.' Lydia glowered at the lively scene.

'I want to see the traction engines in a minute,' said Betty, looking round; but Lydia knew that she really wanted to see Beuno, since it wasn't long since she herself had been in love and she recognised the signs.

'I don't think Elizabeth can be here,' she said, wishing to indicate in a roundabout way that she didn't think Beuno was here either. 'We'd have come across her by now.'

'Hywel's here,' said Betty. 'He's over there at the sheepdog trials, and I saw Wyn and April in the flower arrangement tent.'

'Well, keep out of their way,' said Lydia. 'I don't think I could face Dr Wyn's nudges and winks at the moment.'

'He doesn't mean anything by it,' said

Betty. 'He's probably shy. He's frightened of you. You can be very intimidating.'

Lydia ignored this, although she found it quite flattering. 'Whenever I stand in the middle of a big field,' she said, 'I expect some harpy to come flying at me with a hockey stick. It makes me nervous. Everything that reminds me of school makes me nervous.'

'You're quite safe here,' Betty reassured her.

'I don't like the look of that bull,' said Lydia, 'or that simply colossal pig. If a pig gets its teeth in you it never lets go.'

'That's nonsense,' said Betty. 'If it was true there'd be people all over the world with pigs with their teeth sunk in them.' She stood still and looked across at the beer tent, shading her eyes. 'When you're silly you make everyone else silly,' she told Lydia rebukingly. 'You make me feel all limp and incompetent.'

Lydia felt a bit mean. Perhaps Betty *was* enjoying the occasion. Perhaps she would enjoy it more if Lydia stopped whimpering. 'Let's go and have a beer,' she offered, 'or a hot-dog or some candy-floss.'

'Beer, I think,' said Betty, making for the tent.

'There you are,' said Dr Wyn with strenuous good will.

'So we are,' said Lydia, smiling radiantly.

'Enjoying yourselves?' asked the doctor. 'I had a splendid time in London,' he added, with an air of triumph.

He was like a master of ceremonies, thought Lydia. Or a cheer leader. Incapable of leaving people to get along on their own breathing their own air, thinking their own thoughts.

'What are you drinking?' he asked, going on to apologise that he would have to leave them shortly since it would be time for his surgery.

Betty said sincerely that that was a shame, in order to prevent Lydia from saying it insincerely, as she was clearly about to do. 'Are you having a good time?' she asked April. 'Did your flower arrangement win?'

Disconcertingly, April muttered something incomprehensible and moved a few steps away from them.

'That's not shy,' said Lydia; 'that's just rude. What *have they* been saying about us?'

'I can't think,' said Betty, looking supiciously at Lydia, as though wondering what she had been up to while her own attention had been elsewhere.

'I haven't done a thing,' protested Lydia, reading this look correctly. 'The girl's mad.'

Betty stepped aside and addressed April

purposefully. 'Are your parents here, dear?' she asked in tones that required an answer.

April said 'Yes' unwillingly, but no more.

Lydia was clad in an outfit which like many very beautiful things stopped just short of being ridiculous, hovering on the brink of parody. She had a lot of curly hair and she had tied a bow in it. Her white silk jacket and trousers were of a masculine cut and she looked androgynous and faintly degenerate – an irresistible combination to the sexually confused.

Dr Wyn was highly excited by it and left April's side to whisper an aggressive witticism in Lydia's ear.

'What?' said Lydia loudly. 'Sorry, what did you say?'

He looked at her with detestation, and so did April.

'What was all that about?' asked Betty.

'He was telling me something indelicate about a horse,' said Lydia. 'And all is clear to me. He has told April that I am insanely in love with him, and now they both hate me: he, because I have made it plain this is not the case, and she for much the same reason, only compounded by the fact that since he has raised the subject, and in view of his demeanour towards me... Oh God,

134

I'm getting lost.' Lydia grasped at the air. 'I mean it's the other way round and he is insanely in love with me, and April is mad with him because he is, and she is madder with me because I'm not, since that is so insulting to them both.'

'You always think people are in love with you,' said Betty. 'It's a sign of advancing age or lunacy.'

'No, I don't,' said Lydia, 'do I?'

'You have a tendency that way,' said Betty. 'You are attractive, but people do fall in love with other people, you know.'

'Of course I know,' said Lydia, and at that moment Hywel came among them. He didn't say so, but it was evident that he had been successful in the sheepdog trials, because he was unusually cheerful and forthcoming and he seemed quite jubilant to meet them there.

Lydia greeted him without smiling, which is a chilling expedient, usually employed only after a row has taken place.

He didn't notice. He was drunk, and was finding her interesting again.

'Where's Elizabeth?' asked Betty.

'Elizabeth?' said Hywel. 'Elizabeth. Where's Elizabeth?' He beamed at her, revealing himself to be more drunk than Lydia had first supposed.

'That was enlightening,' said Betty crossly as he turned to speak to another farmer. 'You mustn't flirt with him. He's drunk. I wonder where Elizabeth is.'

Lydia was enraged at the injustice of this and said she was definitely going home now, and what's more her feet were hurting.

Once a person's feet are hurting there is little more to be said, so Betty reluctantly accompanied her to the car.

'Perhaps they'll call in on the way home,' she said wistfully.

Listen, listen, listen. This is what happened. This is what they do. They hurt each other. He said to her, Dr Wyn said to Elizabeth, that he would take her to the Fair. He said Hywel could take the dogs in the van but he would take her in her pretty frock in his clean car. So she put on her pretty frock and the scent that smells of yesterday and Hywel took the dogs in the van and she waited. She sat in the shade of the house wall and she waited, and she knew that I had gone to hide, but she didn't know where. I was crouched in the hay in the stable that the horses have gone from and she didn't know I was watching her. I was thinking 'Poor Elizabeth', because she was happy. She heard the car come up the lane and stepped into the sunlight and her face shone. If I could speak I would have said, 'Elizabeth, Elizabeth, go back into the shadows, get out of the light, hide your shining face in the shadows.'

I knew what he would do. I knew he would bring the girl. The girl who is almost as silent as me and looks at me with such horror. I have watched him before, watched him watching Elizabeth as he puts his arm around a girl. He watches her face and he smiles the way he smiled when I broke my bones. No one but me knows he is smiling because his mouth does not move. But I know. I have seen him with his girls in the fields, and when he knows I am watching he kisses them. The boys from the village kiss their girls when I am there because they do not care, but he only kisses them when he is being watched. He watches and he likes to be watched. If I could I would pull the mountain down on his head and close his smiling eyes.

Elizabeth, poor Elizabeth ran into the sunlight and he stopped the car and he got out and Elizabeth ran towards the car until she saw the girl. I closed my eyes. I do not like to see, things being killed.

She said, 'Angharad is out on the hills alone, so I cannot come to the Fair', and she said, 'I am sorry you have had a wasted journey', and she said, 'Have a nice time at the Fair.'

He said, 'That is a pity,' with his smiling, still mouth, and he got back in the car and drove away, and Elizabeth went back in the house, and all the day she cried, and I went away to the hills.

Elizabeth does not love me, but she does not always hate me, and when she brushes my hair perhaps she means to be kind.

They will go to the concert, Beuno and Elizabeth and Hywel all together, and they will sing; but not Elizabeth, who only hums in the house and who will be watching all the time to see if he is there.

'It's a miracle to me how Hywel got home in that condition,' said Lydia the next day. 'I have seldom seen a person so paralytic.'

'I hope Elizabeth doesn't think we got him like that,' worried Betty. 'I know we shouldn't have let him go, but I didn't feel we know him well enough to tell him he was too drunk to drive.'

'There was a moment when I thought he wasn't going to go ever,' said Lydia. 'I drank all the drink myself so that he couldn't have it, and now I don't feel terribly well.'

'You could've just hidden it,' said Betty.

'I was too tired,' explained Lydia. 'One needs to be very alert to go creeping round with a couple of bottles up one's sleeve, trying to hide them in the coal-scuttle or under the sink.' She yawned. 'I think I'll go and sit in the garden and pull the feathers off the pheasant.'

'What if the gamekeeper sees you?' asked Betty querulously. 'He might arrest you for poaching.'

'I'll say I bought it,' said Lydia.

'You can't say you bought it,' said Betty, speaking now with quiet satisfaction. 'They're out of season.'

'Then I'll say I bought it months ago,' said Lydia. 'I'll say I like them really high.'

There was a hawk pinned to the silken air above the churchyard. Lydia watched it, thinking that they had much in common except that she had her prey in her grasp and was already preparing it for consumption. She wondered if wild creatures were capable of envy, and decided that they were not. Envy was a civilised emotion, attendant upon some degree of security and the possession of things strictly unnecessary to survival. Doubtless the hawk would take her pheasant should she permit it, but its motives would be uncomplicated. Thinking about deadly sin led her to think again of Satan. If you took an 'a' away from his name he would be called 'Stan'. Lydia thought the Prince of Darkness would lose much of his power if everyone habitually called him Stan. She glanced round superstitiously, reflecting that if anyone called her Stan she would determine to get her own back on him.

'Beuno,' she said, as he approached up the path, 'is it altogether wise to be cheeky to the devil?'

'Oh, entirely,' said Beuno without hesitation. 'No other course is possible. If he is afforded the slightest respect it makes him worse, larger.'

'I know you to be right,' said Lydia in her reflective pedantic way, 'but I have not your courage. I might cock a snook at him behind his back but I wouldn't dash into his path making the victory sign.'

'Nor would I,' said Beuno. 'I wouldn't seek him out, but if by mischance he should loom up before me I should waggle my fingers at him.'

'Do you think he knows we're talking about him?' asked Lydia, not nervously, but truly more out of curiosity.

'I don't think he's omnipresent,' said Beuno, 'and he isn't omniscient. He's not the opposite of God, which would mean he'd be as powerful. He has to keep going all the time – to and fro about the world and walking up and down in it. No, I don't think he's listening. His presence is unmistakable...

'The whiff of sulphur?' interrupted Lydia.

'That sort of thing,' said Beuno. 'Very occasionally I have strongly sensed his presence. *His* undoubted presence. But he doesn't need to attend to much personally. His hobgoblins can cause a lot of disruption, and simple ordinary people are remarkably good at being bad.'

'Yes, aren't they,' said Lydia humbly, thinking of herself. 'Are you sure that God is omnipresent?'

'Yes,' said Beuno. 'If God is, he's everywhere, even in the most dreadful situations, rubbing shoulders with Satan.'

'Stan,' said Lydia, abstractedly, pulling away at the feathers of the pheasant and strewing them about her.

'Stan?' queried Beuno.

'It's what I call the devil now,' explained Lydia recalling herself to the conversation. 'I keep wondering what he'd do if I wandered up to the edge of the pit and leaned over and yelled, "Oi, you down there. Stan!"

'I expect he'd gnash his teeth in impotent rage,' said Beuno.

'I would myself,' agreed Lydia.

'What are you talking about?' asked Betty

trotting up rather quickly and eyeing them suspiciously. She had only just seen that Beuno had come and was sitting in the garden amongst the wild Welsh poppies and the camomile daisies and the pheasant feathers. The sight had brought her as swiftly out of the house as a child who sees the ice-cream van.

'I was wondering how to cook this pheasant,' said Lydia mendaciously. 'I was going on about the relative merits of casseroling and roasting. I even wondered whether to make him into soup or pâté.' She didn't know if Betty knew how long Beuno had been there, so endeavoured to give the impression that she could babble away on the topic of cooking game for hours at a time. Betty would have been upset to know that they had been talking of the devil. Then Lydia, the liar, careless kindly liar, looked up and caught Beuno's expression as he watched her; an expression of amused disapprobation. She knew instantly that he was thinking of the Father of Lies – for the Prince of Darkness has as many titles as the Prince of Wales – and she went pink.

Betty, made preternaturally alert by love, saw Beuno looking at Lydia and smiling, but misread his expression. She saw Lydia go pink, and misunderstood. She sat there quietly on the grass and grew very sad.

Oh hell, thought Lydia, moved to unwelcome compassion. Another of the things you can't say is 'Now look here, honeybunch, I know what you think we've been doing, but we *haven't*. Honest.' She went on tearing out feathers, glancing surreptitiously at Betty. After a while, of course, the woebegone aspect of the crossed-in-love becomes very irritating, especially if one is being unjustly blamed for it, so Lydia ripped out the last of the fluff that formed, as it were, the bird's underclothes, rose to her feet gripping her pheasant by its knees, and then bent over and kissed Beuno. The bells of hell went tinga-ling-a-ling.

'The gamekeeper will see those feathers,' said Betty later. 'You should've cleared them away.'

'He'll only think a weasel got it,' said Lydia. Immediately she thought guiltily that if Betty had not been such a nice girl she would now remark acidly that a weasel *had* got it. 'You ought to make Beuno take you to the concert,' she said, thinking instantly that she was being cruelly tactful.

'Beuno doesn't want *me*,' said Betty without rancour. She was washing dishes and seemed quite calm.

Calm to the point of lifelessness, thought Lydia, veering giddily between pity and wrath. 'He wouldn't mind going with you to the concert,' she said, thinking that she could have phrased that better if she'd had more notice.

'Why don't *you* go with him?' asked Betty, carefully rinsing one of Lydia's lustre jugs.

'Because I *hate* good music,' said Lydia. 'You know perfectly well I do. They'll be belting out bits of the *Messiah* and I should go mad.'

'I might go by myself,' said Betty. 'I like to hear them sing.'

'I know,' said Lydia eagerly, relieved to find a topic fit for discussion. 'I can't stand the things they're singing, but like the noise their voices make. If you see what I mean.'

Betty smiled.

It wasn't much of a smile, but it did have a faintly superior tinge to it and Lydia began to feel better. 'It's in the village hall,' she said, 'and there's refreshments at half time. I'll take you there and I'm sure someone will bring you back.' She didn't want to say she was sure Beuno would bring her back because that would make it evident again that she knew the miserable secrets of Betty's heart. 'I'll cook the pheasant while you're out,' she said, 'and eat it before you get home.'

'I'll make the bread sauce if you like,' said Betty selflessly; so Lydia let her, which was fairly unselfish of Lydia who made the best bread sauce in the world with a great deal of butter, nutmeg and black pepper.

Betty was so low that she somehow contrived to hurt her finger quite badly with a clove that she was sticking into an onion. It went down her nail to the quick and the onion juice made it sting.

Lydia was hopeless at first aid. She stood well back, suggesting cold water.

'It's all right,' said Betty courageously. 'I'll put a plaster on it and forget about it.'

'I once had a plaster on my finger,' said Lydia, 'and I was making duck pancakes because an editor and his wife were coming to dinner, and when I'd rolled up all the pancakes I found the plaster was missing.'

'Oh *Lydia,*' said Betty, diverted from her wound.

'I wasn't going to unroll the damn things,' continued Lydia, 'so I banged them in the oven, humming insouciantly the while and served them up all bubbling hot. And then I sat and watched everyone very closely, and after a while I saw Finn chewing and chewing, and then he swallowed it.'

'*Lydia*,' said Betty.

'It was all right,' Lydia reassured her. 'A nice clean cut. No pus or anything. Bit of roughage for him.'

'That's the most disgusting thing I ever heard,' said Betty, but she was smiling.

'It was a bit disgusting,' admitted Lydia, 'but what could I do? Tell everyone to watch out for a foreign body? No one would've eaten anything and my party would've been a flop.'

'You should've told Finn when you saw him chewing,' said Betty.

'How could I?' protested Lydia. "I say, darling, you've got the bit of plaster off my finger." It would've sounded most odd.

'Anyway, a bit of plaster looks very like a bit of duck. He never knew the difference.'

'You're completely unscrupulous, Lydia,' said Betty, but she had laughed for a moment.

Lydia drove Betty to the Village Hall in the evening and drove back alone into the sudden shadow of the hill behind the cottage. Evening fell early over Lydia's garden while

146

the rest of the valley preened itself in the setting sun. She stood watching it while the first bat swept swiftly past her hair.

'Go away,' she said, disconcerted by the sudden alien speed, the urgency of its insect-intent flight.

Then the laughter began.

Lydia was not exactly terrified, but she was sitting very, very still so that if there was the slightest noise she could be quite certain that it was not she who had caused it. Lydia wished any sounds that the night had to offer to be separate and extrinsic from herself. Otherwise she would grow confused as to the limits and the confines of reality, the nature of objectivity and the state of her own mental balance. She had let the fire go out since even the soft fall of ash, the spit of a sudden irritable flame, the shifting of branches in the course of their own attrition filled her ears with restless noise and muffled what might be sounding outside: the soft tread of something moving closer, the susurration of something being unsheathed, the breath of someone hissing through his teeth.

The laughter had stopped a while ago and, ever since, Lydia's imagination had been giving her a hard time. Why, she asked herself, had the laughter ceased? What had stopped being so funny? Had someone or something decided that now was the time to be serious? Surely in time and eternity only death and hell were really serious. She sat on the corner of the old sofa with her legs folded under her and stared at the window, willing the oil lamp not to sputter and distort the sounds that belonged to the night: the true night that lay outside in the garden and the valley and held dominion over the hills. Had she not been nervous, Lydia would have been angry, for she had realised that she was, herself, a domestic beast penned in against the night in a frightening little box of night that was all her own, vulnerable to destruction by the very bounds of its definition. The creatures of the field, unprotected as they were, had yet less to fear from the night, being part of it. Lydia, cooped up like a hen in her house, had branded herself victim, prey, alien and afraid. She told herself that the best thing she could do would be to go out of the house and climb up to where the buzzards and the ravens nested on the cliff top, but she didn't pay herself much attention. It was dark out there.

She was still sitting motionless as a hare

when they returned from the concert.

'You've let the fire go out,' accused Betty.

'I was utterly absorbed in my book,' explained Lydia, wondering where she had left it. 'If you put some firelighters in it'll start again in no time.'

'I was going to make some supper,' said Betty.

'I'll see to the fire,' said Beuno.

'I didn't eat my pheasant,' said Lydia, 'being so absorbed in my book.' She didn't want to explain that she had been too nervous to go in the kitchen and cook it, too lily-livered to turn her back to the window as she lit the gas, too timorous to cause even the tiny sounds of roasting game. 'I shall have it tomorrow.'

'Let me help you,' said Elizabeth to Betty, manifesting a disinclination to sit and make conversation with Lydia.

'I heard someone laughing,' said Lydia, speaking to Beuno but not much caring who heard her. While no one must know the extent to which she had been alarmed, she had no objection to them knowing the cause.

'Not again?' said Betty from the kitchen, rattling pans.

'Yes, again,' said Lydia. 'Peals of it.'

'What does she mean?' Elizabeth asked

Betty. All the villagers had an increasing tendency to address Lydia, if they had to address her at all, in the third person through the medium of Betty and it seemed that Elizabeth too had caught the habit.

'She says she keeps hearing someone laughing,' said Betty.

'What sort of someone?' asked Elizabeth.

Beuno squatting in front of the fire, endeavouring to kindle the kindling said, 'It's all right.'

'What's all right?' asked Lydia.

'She thinks you might think it's Angharad. But she seldom laughs nor ever cries.'

'No, I didn't,' said Elizabeth emerging from the kitchen, 'but she does frighten people sometimes, without meaning to.'

'Only stupid people,' said Lydia, moved to annoyance by Elizabeth's woebegone demeanour. If, as she suspected, Elizabeth was miserable because of that dreary village sawbones, then it was dishonest and unlikeable of her to pretend that it was because of her sister-in-law. And what's more, thought Lydia, anyone with half an ounce of sense would, long since now, have told the doctor in no mean terms what he could go and do with himself.

'You look awfully pale,' she said sharply, as

Elizabeth came into the lamplight, sounding even in her own ears more accusing than sympathetic. There was something about this beaten sort of humility that irritated Lydia almost beyond endurance. She had received a few blows in her time, but after the first shock she had swung back. Never had she limped around like a milk-soaked rabbit, quiet and withdrawn. She suddenly wished that she had Finn here so that she could tell him a few more home truths. She had been frightened, and Lydia hated to be frightened. She burst into song. 'I wish, I wish, I wish in vain, I wish I was a maid again...' she warbled.

'Why on earth are you singing that?' called Betty.

'I don't know,' said Lydia, 'but if you're not awfully good I shall sing it to the end.'

'You should have come to the concert,' said Beuno, getting to his feet.

Lydia laughed. 'I'm not a modest woman,' she said, 'but I know when I'm outclassed.'

Beuno stood and looked at the blaze he had made. 'I like the way you laugh,' he said without coquetry.

'I wish you'd all shut up about laughing,' said Betty with, Lydia noted approvingly, some spirit. 'I'm tired of laughing.' She said supper was ready and rattled the knives and forks.

'I wonder what they used to eat here,' Lydia speculated, 'a hundred years ago.'

'Mutton mostly,' said Beuno. 'Mutton and bread.'

'And mushrooms and blackberries and bilberries,' said Betty.

'And cabbage,' said Beuno. 'Not all countrymen like being countrymen. A lot of them don't like all that countryside or the things that grow in it. That's why the windows of the houses are so small – so that they don't have to see where they've been working all day long. So they can shut it out.'

'I've noticed that,' said Lydia. 'All that Wordsworthian waffle, and then when you meet the people all they want to do is hop on the bus and off to the nearest bright lights.'

'Mam used to make bilberry pie,' said Beuno, 'and sometimes we'd have trout, but her idea of a real treat was tinned salmon and tinned peaches.'

Elizabeth took no part in this discussion and Lydia wondered whether it was her imagination or whether Elizabeth had the air of someone who could say a great deal if she chose. She had certainly taken pains over her dinner party and Hywel had equally certainly shown no enthusiasm for it. How difficult were these culture clashes, especially over the dinner table.

'Some country people like the country,' protested Betty. 'I've met some who do.'

'Of course,' Beuno agreed. 'But on the whole the ones who like it best are the ones who've gone away.'

'Elizabeth likes it,' said Betty encouragingly. 'Don't you, Elizabeth?'

'Yes,' said Elizabeth.

'I think that both the country people and the tourists share to some extent the illusion that the locals dematerialise when the visitors have gone, that all the countryside is a vast TV set to be switched off when no one is watching,' said Beuno.

'You'd rather we'd none of us come, wouldn't you?' said Lydia abruptly.

'How could I,' asked Beuno, 'when I go and return and go again?'

'You could stay,' said Betty.

'Not now the place has changed,' said Beuno. 'Once when all the chapels and the churches were thronged and full of singing I could have stayed because the flock was here, but now I have to go out seeking a flock. It has made me wonder quite often about the calling of shepherd of men. Hywel looks after his sheep because they are here. Would he range the world looking for sheep to care for if there were none here? I don't think so.'

'It's different,' said Betty.

'Not all that different,' said Beuno.

'You think leaving the valley is corrupting, don't you?' said Lydia who was clinging like a terrier to a theme which had occurred to her. 'You think the valley itself is corrupted when strangers visit it.'

'I think you believe that more strongly than I do,' said Beuno. 'My most basic instincts tell me that, but my reason and my God tell me differently. A place, a physical location, is not so different from a graven image. Once you get too exclusive, too obsessed with a place, you are worshipping false gods. I think we may be called upon to wander.'

Lydia thought how the country people sometimes took on the look of the land itself, especially the old: how Angharad seemed more part of the land than of her family. If the land was a graven image then Angharad was its priestess.

'I'm confused now,' she said. 'I *think* I think that tourists should be banned except for me. I think that's what I think, but I'm not sure that if I'd been born here I'd be pleased to see me walking down the lane. I think I should regard me with the contempt with which I myself regard the more vulgar visitors.'

'Well, there is that,' said Beuno, 'of course. But there is also envy and fear of where you have been and what you have done.'

'I always say you can be frightening, Lydia,' said Betty.

'I don't mind being frightening,' said Lydia. 'But I should hate to think that I was intrusive.'

Hywel came home alone. He had been singing, and when he came in he came in singing. He only sings when the house is empty. He looked to see that I was asleep, as he used to do before Elizabeth came, and he sang as he used to do before Elizabeth came. Elizabeth who was bright and full of laughter has brought silence with her. She has stolen me from Hywel, and the house from Hywel and all the song from Hywel. The women in the village say, 'Poor Elizabeth, she has a lot to put up with, with that big old house and Angharad, and Hywel working so hard on the farm,' but their eyes gleam as they speak and they do not like her. Sometimes I like her. Sometimes I think 'Poor Elizabeth'. And if

I could cry I would.

'Good heavens,' said Lydia. 'Rock drawings. How very peculiar.'

'Where?' asked Betty, her tone sceptical.

'Here,' said Lydia.

'Good heavens,' said Betty.

They stared at the flat blade of rock jutting out of the turf-clad flank of the hill.

'Perhaps they're druidical,' said Betty hopefully.

'Don't be daft,' said Lydia. 'The men are wearing jackets and trousers and the women have got short skirts. I think the druids were clad mainly in woad.'

'But who would come out here to scribble on rock?' asked Betty unanswerably.

Lydia didn't answer. She was peering closely at the drawings. 'One of them's got a stethoscope,' she said. 'Several of them have got a stethoscope. I think it's all the same man, only the females are all different. What an odd thing. Oops.'

'What?' said Betty.

'Don't look,' said Lydia. 'It's rude.'

'Dear, oh, dear,' said Betty, who naturally had looked. 'It is a bit.'

'They're rather good drawings,' said Lydia. 'Simple but effective.'

'I don't like that one,' said Betty distastefully.

'It isn't actually prurient,' said Lydia, gazing at it. 'More sort of clinical. Dispassionate observation.'

'Some things are better not observed,' said Betty.

'There's a theory that anyone who has witnessed the act depicted here is incurable,' said Lydia.

'Incurable from what?' enquired Betty.

'From the neurosis induced by witnessing the act depicted here,' explained Lydia. 'Though put like that it all sounds a bit circular. And anyway, when you think of what goes on on telly now, if it was true we'd all be raving.'

'I very seldom watch telly,' said Betty.

'Nor do I, pet,' said Lydia indulgently. 'Only sometimes when I'm tired it sort of forces itself on my attention.' She sat down and leaned back against the rock looking out over the sweep of moorland. 'If we had a dog we could let it off the leash now and it would go and roll in the heather.'

'No, we couldn't,' said Betty. 'It might chase sheep.'

'I would have trained it not to do so,' said Lydia. 'I should be very firm with it.'

Betty began to open her mouth to argue that it wasn't well trained at all until she remembered that it didn't exist, and she had vowed not to get drawn into Lydia's idiotic fantasies.

Lydia grinned to herself. She had grown fond of Betty and found her thought-processes amusing.

'You've sat on a bilberry,' said Betty with satisfaction. 'Your trousers are stained.'

'I don't care,' said Lydia. 'It's too pretty a day to mind about such things.'

'You could dye them the same colour,' said Betty. 'You can make dyes from heather.'

Lydia said life was too short to mess about making dyes from heather. It was easier to buy a new pair of pants.

'I'd quite like to try making my own dye,' said Betty. 'It would be very rewarding.'

'Speaking of self-sufficiency,' said Lydia, 'I still haven't eaten that perishing pheasant. I shall have it as soon as we go back.'

'It's horribly high,' warned Betty. 'I smelled it when I opened the cupboard this morning.'

'Then I'll go at once and cook it,' said Lydia who was adamantly determined not to be thwarted of her bird. She broke into a run as they returned to the cottage.

It was high. There was no denying it. Lydia even went so far as to bathe it in vinegar at Betty's behest.

'Faugh,' said Betty, waving her fingers in front of her nose like an eighteenth-century character in a costume drama. 'It stinks.'

'Rubbish,' said Lydia, resolutely sticking a lump of butter in it.

It smelled all right when she got it out of the oven. She left it to settle on top of the stove while she warmed up some bread sauce and crisps. Betty discouraged a fly from sitting on it and watched it as she prepared a salad for herself.

Lydia wasn't actually desperately hungry but she managed to eat most of the pheasant, making vulgar noises of gastronomic appreciation.

'You are *disgusting*,' reproved Betty, toying daintily with a dandelion leaf.

No one called that evening, and they went to bed early.

Lydia woke suddenly in the tangible blackness that was moonless country night. There were unusual sounds in the house. She reached down to the floor where her candle stood, and when she'd groped for the matches, which proved, as always, astonishingly difficult to locate, she lit it.

Betty was being sick. Or, if it wasn't Betty, *someone* certainly was. Lydia felt her way to the door of the tiny bathroom. 'Are you all right?' she asked in the lowered tone that one uses in the darkness. Stupid question.

'Oh, I'm so sick,' came a wail after a moment from the other side of the door.

'Oh, poor you,' said Lydia inadequately, suddenly ripped with a desire, which she recognised as utterly reprehensible, to sit on the floor and giggle insanely. It was so deeply, wholly unfair. And so characteristic of life.

'It can't've been anything I ate,' said poor Betty later, as she sat shivering by the kitchen table while Lydia kindly boiled some water for her. 'It must be a virus I picked up somewhere.'

'You were lucky to make it to the lav,' observed Lydia, meaning that she was very grateful that Betty had made it to the lav, since one of the rules is that the afflicted person does not mop up her own vomit and Lydia was absolutely no good at doing this. Sick made her sick. Even now she stood further from Betty than was entirely necessary. Still, seeing the poor girl shivering so, Lydia did go and fetch her dressing-gown.

160

'Oh, you are kind, Lydia,' said Betty, making Lydia feel like a skunk. 'I'm a bit better now. I think I'll go back to bed.'

'Take a bucket with you,' advised Lydia, not solicitously, just to be on the safe side.

Betty thanked her for the bucket and smiled at her, and Lydia, who, if Betty went on like this, might turn out to be quite human, decided that she would take her her breakfast in bed in the morning: thin crispy toast with a scraping of butter and golden clear jasmine tea, and an egg-cupful of harebells to remind her of the sky.

'You're an angel,' said Betty next morning, as Lydia, with meticulous deliberation, carried out her vow.

It was *all* unfair, reflected Lydia. Betty doing this sort of thing was simply taken for granted, whereas when a nasty, selfish, attractive person like Lydia did it people grew breathless with thanks. 'You stay in bed,' she said. 'I'll go down to the village and see if they've got any newspapers and magazines.'

At this Betty's eyes widened with wondering gratitude and Lydia felt unworthy. She also felt the beginnings of wrath. Days ago she had decided to be good – she was being quite good – but she was only pretending to be good so far and all this appreciation was as yet undeserved. She wondered how long she would have to keep it up before she could stop convicting herself of hypocrisy.

'Shall I get the doctor to come and see you?' she asked, and was surprised when Betty said she thought it might be a good idea.

'I feel so giddy now,' Betty explained apologetically. 'My head keeps going round.'

Dr Wyn came at lunchtime while Lydia was eating pheasant leg and wondering whether the goodness inherent in a broth made from pheasant carcase was sufficient to justify sneaking it, disguised as *soupe bonne femme,* on to the supper tray of an ailing vegetarian, and what her real motives were.

'She was very sick,' Lydia told him coldly. 'She's upstairs in bed feeling giddy.'

He banged his head on the beam at the top of the stairs.

Lydia heard the concussion. 'Physician heal thyself,' she remarked *sotto voce.*

When he came down he was wearing a professional air and said the symptoms were those of food poisoning.

For some reason, although she had not been doing the cooking, this made Lydia feel like Lucretia Borgia. 'How could it be?'

she asked. 'She only eats salads and things. And mushrooms. Maybe she got a funny mushroom.'

'Just give her liquids for a time,' he said and dropped his professional air.

Lydia eyed him discouragingly. He had sighed, rubbed his hands together and sat down on a kitchen chair. Now he reached out and picked up a pheasant wing which he proceeded to eat.

Lydia watched incredulously. 'I'm surprised you're not frightened to eat that,' she said, 'in this pestilent household.'

'Oh, I trust you,' he said. 'You wouldn't poison me.'

Oh, I might, thought Lydia, but she said: 'I didn't poison Betty either,' in a childishly defensive way which put her in a worse mood.

'Elizabeth and Beuno were here last night as well,' she said. 'Perhaps you'd better go and have a look at them. They could be writhing round in agony.'

'They'd've let me know,' he said, picking up another splinter of pheasant.

Exasperatedly, Lydia filled the kettle. This man was the opposite of Beuno, who followed her thoughts with ease, needed no explanations and leapt to no wrong conclusions. To converse with the doctor she would have to speak with unnatural care and lucidity, and she really couldn't be bothered.

He tipped his chair back and fixed his gaze full upon her, very much at home. 'I'd love a cup of tea, thanks,' he said. 'Or possibly something a bit stronger.'

'I haven't got anything stronger,' said Lydia. 'I've got to go down to the off-licence later.'

'Never mind,' he said. 'You're intoxicating enough.'

Lydia ignored this. 'I'd better go and see how Betty is,' she said.

'Don't go,' he said. 'Talk to me.'

He too sounded childish, Lydia realised, reflecting that childishness in an adult was painfully unattractive. 'I have a great deal to do,' she said in a dismissively grown-up voice.

For a moment it seemed that he would protest, but then he got up.

'Goodbye,' said Lydia going rapidly upstairs.

She looked out of the little window above the door and saw him stop on the path. Elizabeth appeared out of the overhanging leaves and confronted him. That was the way it was, thought Lydia – she *confronted* him. I was right, she said to herself. Clever old me.

'Lydia,' called Betty, 'is that you?'

'It is I,' said Lydia, opening the bedroom door. 'How are you feeling?'

'A bit weak,' said Betty, 'but better. I just had a funny thought. You know those rock drawings. Well, when Wyn had his stethoscope in his ears I wondered if they were meant to be him. Perhaps I'm delirious. It could've been any doctor, and it might not've been a stethoscope. It might have been a necklace.'

'People don't stick necklaces in their ears,' said Lydia thoughtfully. 'I think you're right. How perceptive we're all getting.'

'No, I must be wrong,' said Betty. 'It's the sort of silly idea one gets when one's ill.'

'It's the sort of silly idea I get all the time,' observed Lydia, 'only this time it was you who got it.'

'But who would've made the drawings?' asked Betty.

'Some discarded mistress?' surmised Lydia. 'Some cuckolded person?'

Betty persisted, 'No, but why would they go all that way to draw on a rock?'

Lydia considered, 'You mean, why not

squirt rude messages on the petrol station?'

'Not quite that,' said Betty. 'It just seems odd to do it where no one is likely to see it. It doesn't seem like revenge.'

No, thought Lydia, it didn't. The drawings had had that oddly unimpassioned quality. None of the fetid rage of the sexually wronged.

'What a mysterious valley this is,' she said. 'Unexplained laughter and filthy drawings in secret places. Perhaps Stan is walking abroad.'

'Who?' asked Betty.

'Oh, no one,' said Lydia. 'Perhaps the ancient fairies are looking after things round here.'

The woman from Ty Fach has found the pictures that I made on the rock, and the little woman with her has looked at them. I lay in the bracken on the side of the hill and watched them. I did not think that anyone would ever see the pictures except the sheep and the swooping ravens. I thought that I would scratch out the pictures, but now that the woman has seen them they are not mine any more. They have moved from the rock into her eyes and into her head and so they are hers. There is little that is mine. No, no, no. The hills are mine, and the living streams and the wind that breathes in the valley and the tiny white flowers that only I know because only I lie so close to the earth that I can see them move. I lie so close to the earth that I am part of it and so it is mine. And once I remember – I very faintly remember – that I flew as the buzzards and the ravens fly and all the great sky was mine. I have been dead for a long time and by day I circle the huge air above the hills and by night I sleep in the quiet rock, as quiet as the rock, and the little worms mean consolation as they eat me.

Lydia was tired of being good. She felt it didn't altogether suit her. It made her feel a little dowdy, as though she had taken up residence in the suburbs of morality. Had she had it in her to be extraordinarily good she would have felt cosmopolitan, since, she considered, there was a definite elegance, a *chic*, in sanctity. Being a mere apprentice was boring and carried no *cachet*, and Lydia was dauntedly aware that she had a long way to go before she achieved the skills and ease of perfection. It was much, much easier to be mischievous, to be slightly bad; and while, of course, being very good was an infinity, an eternity, away from being very bad, being a bit bad was very similar to being a bit good and unfortunately offered more opportunities for fun.

'Let's have a picnic,' she said, telling herself that next week she would make a real effort to work again at the practice of virtue.

Betty was enthusiastic. 'A real one,' she cried. 'An Edwardian one with tablecloths and lobster patties and champagne.'

'I was thinking more in terms of sardine sandwiches and a flask of tea,' said Lydia. 'The village shop is short on lobster and I don't see why I should pour Dom Perignon down people's gullets.' Nevertheless she spoke mildly. 'Anyway,' she said, 'the Molesworths would turn up their noses at anything too fancy. They like sort of hotel tea.'

Betty was astonished. 'Do you mean to ask the Molesworths?' she asked. 'I thought you couldn't stand them.'

This threw Lydia into some perplexity. She was not so far gone in the sinful practice of dissimulation that she felt free to claim that she meant to ask them because she knew Betty would be pleased, and she could think of no other remotely credible reason for doing so.

'I knew you'd like me to ask them,' she said eventually, since there was nothing else for it. 'I shan't have to talk to them because we'll be running round in the fresh air and there's no very formal *placement* for picnics.'

'I think it's very nice of you,' said Betty. 'They'll be awfully pleased.'

It isn't at all nice of me, thought Lydia, and they won't be pleased, but they'll come from curiosity and snobbery, since although they don't approve of me they think I'm rather posh. 'We *will* make it a nice picnic,' she said, in the spirit of the penitent who intends to do the wicked thing she had first thought of but will also do something pleasant to make it slightly less reprehensible. Dimly she heard the bells of hell distantly pealing. 'Let's have egg sandwiches,' she said hurriedly, 'and cucumber and ham. And China tea and white wine, and you can make a cake. We'll take the car to the foot of the mountain and walk from there.'

'Lovely,' said Betty, sighing with innocent delight. 'We'll take fruit as well and I can make a quiche.'

'You mustn't do too much,' said Lydia, misguidedly, as Betty took this for further evidence of her good-heartedness; 'you haven't been well.'

'I'm fine now,' claimed Betty. 'It was just a touch of summer flu or something. Now, who exactly are we asking?'

'Elizabeth,' said Lydia, 'and Beuno and the doctor and April and April's Mum and Dad.'

'Not Hywel?' asked Betty.

'We can ask him,' said Lydia, 'but he won't come. Farmers don't go on picnics. I somehow know they don't. I can't picture a farmer on a picnic. They used to have bread and cheese and a jug of cider under the hedgerow, but I don't think they even do that any more. I think they jump in the jeep and go home for mince and dumplings and a mug of instant coffee.'

I know now that I always knew that the woman would find the pictures. I knew when I saw her in the graveyard reading the writing. She likes to know. People who like to know make the earth smaller. I would like to see the earth grow and everything in the earth grow until it touched the skirts of heaven, and no one could be dead.

'She's a very interesting study,' said Dr Wyn. 'She is not without intelligence, but the harm that was done to her at birth is irreversible.' He had called, ostensibly, to check on the state of Betty's health but now had his feet under the table in no uncertain fashion.

Lydia thought that the harm done to us all

on being born was irreversible but held her tongue.

Dr Wyn tilted his chair and leaned towards the dresser. Stretching out his arm he took Finn's postcard in his fingertips and settled his chair back on to an even keel. He scrutinised the picture and then turned it over to study the postmark, or possibly, thought Lydia, to read the message. 'Greece, hmmm,' he remarked.

'Would you like some more tea?' asked Betty in a hurry. She knocked over a cup in her haste to defuse this touchy situation.

'Love some,' said Dr Wyn, putting the postcard on the table. Lydia picked it up, wondering whether to clutch it possessively to her chest, her arms crossed over it like a person in an old melodrama.

'His manners,' she said indignantly, when he had reluctantly left, peering at his watch and bemoaning the urgency of surgery hours. 'The way he makes himself at *home*.'

'He doesn't mean to be rude,' explained Betty. 'He wants to seem at ease and be friendly.'

'He hasn't got it right then,' snapped Lydia. 'He hasn't got it right at all. He called me his old darling at one point. Ooh, I was cross.'

Even Betty knew that this would be difficult to excuse. Nevertheless she had a go. 'You can't expect a lot of polish in a country GP,' she said.

'I don't expect a lot of polish,' protested Lydia. 'I just expect not to be leered at and not to have my correspondence read. It isn't a lot to ask.'

Betty pressed on. 'I know he only means to be friendly and appear relaxed.'

Lydia regarded her keenly. 'I can't think why you're so determined to defend him,' she said in the tone of one on the verge of enlightenment.

'I'm sorry for him,' said Betty unexpectedly. 'Sometimes he looks like a poor little child outside a cake shop.'

As this was precisely the aspect of him which Lydia found most annoying the discussion lapsed.

That evening Lydia called at Château Molesworth to proffer her picnic invitation. She wore a babyish frock with little pink flowers embroidered on it and the gentle charm which she used on people who might be frightened of her.

April opened the door and was clearly both astonished and displeased to see her there.

'Hullo,' said Lydia without originality but with appealing warmth.

As she expected, April accepted her invitation. Her expression softened when Lydia said that she would like her parents to come too, and again Lydia had misgivings. To quell them she said that April was looking very pretty in her yellow track suit. She *was* actually looking quite pretty, but Lydia didn't think so. She thought that April looked as though she bought all her clothes from a catalogue. 'That colour does suit you,' she said. And it did quite, but bad Lydia didn't know because she had made up her mind already and was blind to the simpler aspects of reality.

What remained of her conscience ached a little as she drove home remembering that, if she cared to, she could make April love her, and that this was a dangerous, potentially harmful ability. Beuno who had a similar quality, she knew, did not misuse it. If she had still been in love with Finn, Lydia would not now be casting round for ways to entertain herself. Love was like water. Out of control it caused dreadful havoc, but when it ran smoothly and sweetly it not only modified life's aridity but added a pleasing dimension to the view, while Lydia, at present, was using it only to make mud pies. She felt suddenly depressed, as though a darkness lay upon her. She was morose and silent when she got home.

'What *is* the matter?' asked Betty. 'Did they say they wouldn't come?' She couldn't remember ever seeing Lydia so cast down. 'Were they rude to you?'

'No,' said Lydia, 'they were delighted.' She poured herself a drink and stood by the door watching the innocent evening settle on the graveyard.

'Why are you so quiet?' asked Betty after a while. 'I hope you haven't caught whatever it was I had.'

'I wish I wasn't having a picnic,' said Lydia. 'I wish I'd never thought of it. I wish Beuno would call.' She wished she was a better person. That was what she really wished.

'I expect he will,' said Betty. If the presence of Beuno was all that would cheer up Lydia then Betty felt that he should be here. Lydia morose seemed a painfully unnatural phenomenon. Her misery blackened the evening and should be assuaged at all costs. 'I'm going to light the candles,' Betty said, 'so do close the door or the moths will fly in.'

'I'm waiting for the laughter,' said Lydia.

174

'If it comes tonight I shall track it down.'

Beuno came first and then the laughter. As soon as Lydia saw him she realised that she could have her picnic without putting her wicked plan into operation. She merely had to change the venue slightly. She couldn't think why she hadn't thought of that before. It would make the whole exercise entirely pointless, but she didn't care. She had been about to collude with Stan in the face of all her good resolutions, and there would have been yet another indelible stain on her spirit which, she suspected, were it available to her, she would not care to put unwashed in her underwear drawer. Perhaps that was what mothers meant when they insisted you should change your underwear daily for fear you should be run over. Lydia knew that, whereas her lingerie was impeccable, her spirit would not stand up well to close inspection in the event of an accident.

Betty was so relieved to see Lydia in spirits again that she didn't care at all that it was Beuno who had wrought the transformation. She was beginning to realise that whatever Lydia felt for Beuno was different in kind from what she had felt for Finn, and this had eased her incipient unhappiness, for while it is one thing not to win the beloved it is another to see him swept off by somebody else, and far, far worse.

'Why is Dr Wyn such a pain in the back of the neck?' asked Lydia.

'*Lydia*,' said Betty.

'No, but he is,' said Lydia. 'He's socially insecure and he presumes too much and he ate half my pheasant. Beuno doesn't mind if I speak truthfully. Truth is his business. Tell me why the man is as he is.'

'I will if you want me to,' said Beuno.

'I implore you to,' said Lydia. 'I wish to widen my already profound understanding of human nature. Why is he still here, so discontented in his native village?'

'His mother wouldn't let him leave,' said Beuno. 'She didn't look like one of the village matriarchs – she was quite small – but she might have been quarried out of the local slate. She was determined he should qualify as a doctor and just as determined that he should practise here. She told him that he had to be successful and then she made it impossible for him. Some country GPs enjoy the life, I suppose, but he wanted to go.'

'That's a very good method of driving people mad,' said Lydia. 'Telling them to do something, then arranging matters so that they can't.'

'There was more to it than that,' said Beuno after a while. 'He had a brother like Angharad and his mother was determined that Wyn should help look after him. She was – not ashamed of him – but outraged that one of her children should be like that. We're all related, you know, but Wyn's mother thought herself superior. She was unhappy all her life.'

'Where are they now?' asked Betty. 'Wyn's mother and brother.'

'Dead,' said Beuno.

'Then why doesn't he hop it?' demanded Lydia.

'It's too late,' said Beuno. 'If he went now he would see all his previous life here as a waste of time, and in a way he is wreaking vengeance on his mother by being embittered and something of a failure – saying, look what you've done to me.'

'I once had a sort of vague idea that life in the country was innocent and uncomplicated,' said Lydia. 'I am familiar with the darker view which encompasses bestiality, incest, parricide, rustling, infanticide and the murderous rivalry within the Women's Institute, but I had imagined that this view was the product of a warped approach to life and greatly exaggerated.'

'Sometimes in a small community – and ours is very small – passions which in a wider context would be dissipated become distilled and reduced to poison. A trivial slight, a threat to self-esteem, which might cause you a moment's irritation, here can give rise to resentments which may fester for centuries.' Beuno smiled at her. 'The only peace that you'll find here lies in a kind of pagan solitude.'

'Where's God?' asked Lydia, rather petulantly.

'Here, of course,' said Beuno. 'But no more here than anywhere else. You'll find him just as easily on Paddington Station if you happen to be looking.'

'It's all very depressing,' said Lydia reverting to the topic of the doctor. 'I always think of doctors as plumbers, but they don't usually see themselves like that. They mostly think they're marvellous and act lordly and gallop about being pillars of the community.'

'Poor man,' said Betty. 'Supper's ready.'

'I'm frightfully hungry,' said Lydia, making Betty feel useful. 'What is for supper?'

It was carrot soup and salad of course, but it wasn't bad and they drank cider with it.

'Perhaps we could have cider with our

picnic,' said Betty. 'It's cheaper than wine.'

'I don't like it as much,' said Lydia, 'but perhaps it would be more suitable. More rustic and in keeping with the occasion.'

'Shall I make some sausage rolls?' asked Betty.

'You are very ambivalent about the sausage,' Lydia accused her. 'Do you love him or do you hate him? One minute you say trustfully that he contains only soya meal and the next you suspect him of harbouring chunks of minced-up nameless anatomy. You must make your position clear.'

'I think a lot depends on the make,' said Betty. 'The known brands must have a certain proportion of meat in them, but I don't know what sort. And the others could have almost anything, but I think it's mostly cereal. I don't think I will make sausage rolls. I'll make some anchovy savouries instead.'

'I think you're wise,' said Lydia. 'Let us stay on the safe side. We want no repetition of the other evening.'

'Oh ho,' agreed Betty, shuddering. 'I felt terrible.'

'She was sick,' explained Lydia to Beuno.

'Yes, I heard,' said Beuno. 'Wyn told me.'

'What has he done with his Hippocratic oath?' asked Lydia severely. 'Whatever happened to confidentiality?'

'He sees himself more as your friend than your doctor,' explained Beuno.

'Does he?' said Lydia. She leaned her head on her hand and stirred her cider with a fingertip. They sat on in friendly silence until the laughter began, whereat Lydia's glass shook beneath her hand.

'What is it?' asked Betty, startled.

'Listen,' said Lydia. 'Listen.'

'It's the wind,' said Betty after a while uncertainly.

'There is no wind,' said Lydia. Those branches still just visible in the encroaching night were motionless.

'It's laughter,' said Beuno. He got up and opened the door. 'But I can't tell where it's coming from.'

Lydia was now no longer frightened. If Beuno could hear the laughter it could not, in her estimation, be bad; nor could she be mad. She stalked, stiff-legged like a wolf, into the darkling garden and like a wolf she sniffed the air.

Betty followed, straining her ears. 'Where is it?' she fussed. 'I can hardy hear a thing.'

'It's all over,' said Lydia. 'That's what's so odd. It comes from everywhere.'

'I can hear *something*,' conceded Betty, 'but

it does sound to me like wind or water.'

Lydia sucked her finger and held it up. 'No wind,' she repeated after a moment.

'There may be a wind further down the valley,' said Betty. 'You know how sheltered we are here.'

'It's someone laughing,' said Lydia. 'Roars of laughter.'

'I think you've made yourself hear it,' said Betty. 'The way one used to do in trains. They'd say anything that you had on your mind – licketty split, licketty split, or ticketty boo, ticketty boo...'

'I never in my life heard a train say licketty split or tickety boo,' protested Lydia. 'But anyway this isn't like that.'

'Beuno,' called Betty. 'What do you make of it?'

Beuno was on the far side of the stream, his head inclined towards the graveyard. He turned to face her. 'It's someone laughing,' he said.

'Oh, you're as bad as each other,' said Betty, disappointed in him. 'You're usually so sensible.'

'Not very sensible,' he said, walking back towards her. He pointed at his feet. 'I walked in the stream.'

'You'd better come back in the house and

dry your shoes and socks,' said Betty. 'No sense in getting rheumatism or pneumonia.' She pushed open the door and stood still on the threshold. 'It's stopped,' she said.

'I don't know how you know it's stopped if you couldn't hear it,' said Lydia, 'but you're quite right. It has stopped.'

'I could hear something,' said Betty. 'It just didn't sound to me like laughter. What an odd thing.'

'I mean to get to the bottom of it,' said Lydia, only without much conviction. 'This is one of the things I would prefer to understand.'

'The only really profound question,' said Beuno, 'is *why*. *How* is a question asked by the foolish and answered by the trivial.'

'Are you telling me off?' enquired Lydia good-humouredly.

'Of course not,' said Beuno. 'It's just one of the things I like to point out sometimes. I don't always get the chance.'

'The sooner you're ordained the better,' said Lydia. 'If you have this passion for pointing things out to people there could be no finer way of gratifying it than from the pulpit.'

'Do come on in,' said Betty. 'I'm going to stoke up the fire and dry Beuno's socks.'

'Like Mary Magdalene,' said Lydia. 'Not that she ever dried Beuno's socks, but you see what I mean.'

'No, I don't a bit see what you mean,' said Betty. 'You're being silly again.'

'I don't think you should be frightened,' said Beuno.

'I'm not,' said Lydia quickly.

Beuno went on. 'Laughter and evil can't coexist. There's nothing funny in hell.'

'It's not just evil that frightens people,' Lydia reminded him. 'Jehovah was wont to scare the pants off the Israelites – or whatever it was they girded up their loins with.'

'Only when they were naughty,' said Beuno comfortingly.

'The fact that in saying that you clearly mean to reassure me,' said Lydia, 'shows that you do not know me at all well. Anyway, fashions in mirth change. People used to go to Bedlam to laugh at the lunatics. Not funny. And I don't think slapstick is funny. I hate seeing plates being broken. I hate mess. Humour comes out of precision, not chaps. That's why nuclear war is so frightening – like slapstick. Destruction and confusion. And just *think* of the breakage. I wonder if on some distant planet there are creatures who are holding their sides at the prospect of us hurling plates at each other.'

'Although,' said Beuno thoughtfully, 'the Second Law of Thermodynamics is extremely funny because all the things we are all so busy doing only hasten the inevitable end. Earnest misapprehension is very funny.'

'Perhaps we've got more sophisticated,' said Lydia. 'People slipping on banana skins aren't funny, but people spending a lifetime trying to figure out the meaning of the banana are. Especially when the banana goes off in their hand.'

'Do try to think of something more cheerful,' said Betty. 'You're making me depressed.'

The woman from Ty Fach came here tonight with Beuno.

She said, 'Elizabeth, come to my picnic,' and her voice ran with honey. And she said, 'Hywel, will you come to my picnic?' and her voice ran with laughter.

'Picnic,' said Hywel, and he said softly as he went away, 'Diawl take picnics.'

The woman said, 'How nice it is here in the evening. How pretty this room is. Is it you, Elizabeth, who has made it so pleasant?'

Sometimes I can hear Elizabeth smile, even before I hear the smile changing the shape of her

184

voice. If Hywel said to her the things the woman says, for a time Elizabeth would smile.

Then I heard Hywel come back into the room and the smiling stopped.

'Do come to my picnic,' the woman said, and her voice sounded as her silk scarf sounds when it trails behind her through the branches in the wood.

Hywel is silent and Beuno speaks, but I do not hear what he says.

There is a mouse above me in the roof and I am going to listen to it.

'They're all coming except Hywel,' said Lydia as she returned later that evening. 'I told you he wouldn't. The farmhouse was even more grim than usual tonight. I can't think what it must be like when Beuno isn't there. I shouldn't think they ever speak at all.'

'Most married couples don't talk all that much,' said Betty.

'Yes, but what they don't say probably wouldn't frizzle your ears if they said it,' explained Lydia, not at her most lucid. 'What is left unsaid in the farmhouse is positively hair-raising. I am myself now quite certain that Hywel knows about Elizabeth and the doctor. His silence has just that quality of wrath and frustration.'

Betty sat up. 'Ssshh,' she said. 'Anyone might hear you.'

'Who?' asked Lydia reasonably. 'Owls and bats and mice and the phantom laugher, I suppose.'

But Betty also knew that there are some things better left unsaid, no matter what the circumstances. Perhaps Hywel in his silence was proving wise. She said so.

Lydia thought about it for a while, before she spoke. 'What you're saying is,' she said, 'that one shouldn't even whisper it in the wind on the hill tops because once said a thing can never be unsaid; that expression gives power to thought; that even the clear though unspoken formulation of a nebulous impression may be dangerous, giving it a force and potency which silence or merely a lack of clarification would deny to it.'

'Yes,' said Betty after about half a minute.

'I think I agree with you,' said Lydia after a further half a minute.

Sometimes I hear shots in the night. Dead metal speeding into fur and feathers and flesh to make things dead. And sometimes Hywel goes out in the day with his gun and he shoots rabbits and pigeons and crows and foxes, and some he brings home to eat, and some he hangs in the hedges to remind the world that there is death. Once Elizabeth used to say, 'Oh Hywel, Hywel, I cannot skin that rabbit. The poor little thing,' and he would laugh, and sometimes he would skin it himself and sometimes he would throw it away, but now she says, 'I am not going to skin that rabbit, Hywel, so don't imagine I am,' and sometimes he skins it himself and sometimes he throws it away. Tonight I hear shouts. The woman from Ty Fach is laughing and shouting in the night.

Betty had heard the car stop in the lane and had begun to frighten herself even before she heard someone slip in the stream and swear, long before the knock on the door.

'What the hell?' said Lydia, leaning indignantly out of the window over the door, like Rapunzel with a hair-cut.

'For God's sake let me in,' said Finn. 'I fell in that bloody stream and I'm drenched.'

Lydia gave a screech of eldritch mirth. 'I *knew* you'd be back,' she crowed. 'Go away.'

Betty who had nearly died of fear now felt almost dead with relief and crept to Lydia to remonstrate with her. 'You can't turn him away at this hour,' she said. 'Where would he go?'

'Yes, where would I go?' demanded the man standing in the garden. 'Who's that?' he asked. 'Make Lydia see sense, will you?'

'It's me. Betty,' said Betty over Lydia's shoulder, which was shaking because she was still laughing.

'Tell her to let me in,' demanded Finn.

'You must let him in,' said Betty.

'No, I mustn't,' said Lydia. She stopped laughing. 'There's a lot of ducks over there by the stream,' she said. 'They'd be delighted to see you, I'm sure.' She slammed down the window and told Betty to go back to bed.

'Oh *Lydia*,' said Betty, not for the first time. She opened the window again. 'Finn,' she said, 'try the village shop. They do bed and breakfast, and the pub may not be full. They're probably used to people calling in the middle of the night.'

'I don't think they're used to people calling in the middle of the night,' said Lydia, beginning to laugh again. 'They'll tell him to go to hell.'

'You're mean, Lydia,' said Betty. 'You're cruel.'

'You're fucking mad, Lydia. You know that?' came a parting shout from the garden.

Lydia flew back to the window, flung it up and said some further things into the darkness of the middle of the night.

'*Lydia*,' said Betty. 'If anyone heard you...'

'Who could hear me?' asked Lydia crossly. 'Anyway, I don't care. The unmitigated gall of the man, strolling up at this time and expecting a welcome. Not to mention the fact that he has been conspicuously faithless to me. How dare he come back.'

'He probably loves you really,' said Betty.

'He probably does,' said Lydia, 'but he's blown it.' All the bells of hell rang out in a wild cacophony.

'Oh *Lydia*,' said Betty again, 'you shouldn't be so unforgiving. It's worse than Finn going away. It's worse than infidelity.'

'I daresay,' said Lydia, 'but hell could freeze over before I'd have him back.'

She lay awake till dawn thinking about it. She was delighted that Finn had returned to give her the opportunity of rejecting him. She was determined that there would be no reconciliation, and even though she had found that the sound of his voice reminded her vividly and immediately that she had loved him and could do so again she lay smiling with pleasure at the sheer satisfaction of unforgivingness. It was, she decided, much sweeter than love: a sensation for the connoisseur of emotion. That it was also wicked did not greatly perturb her. It was a sin different in kind from mischief-making and could, in Lydia's estimation, be excused on the grounds that it was the sexual mis-behaviour of another to which she was re-sponding.

Lydia felt strongly that the author of the universe probably thought much as she did about sexual matters. She really did have a long way to go, and she had not yet learned to recognise the precise lineaments, the demeanour and the shape of the shadow of Stan.

Elizabeth made him come to the farmhouse. He came when Hywel was here and the men and Beuno were in the yard. She was waiting in the yard and she said, 'I want you to look at Angharad. Let us go inside where we can talk in peace.' And when they were inside she said in a different voice, 'What is going on between you and that girl?'

He said, 'What girl?'

She said, 'You know what girl. April, May, June, July...'

He said, 'For God's sake, Elizabeth, what is wrong with you? I just gave her lift to the Fair.'

'You've taken her out,' said Elizabeth. 'I heard them in the shop talking and they said you had

taken her out.'

He said, 'Oh, once or twice maybe. There's nothing in it, Elizabeth.'

She said, 'I don't believe you.'

He said, 'Oh, for God's sake.'

And she said, 'They said that her mother had told them you would marry.'

'You know how they talk,' he said. He sounded angry, but he was smiling. He is a little afraid of Elizabeth, but he loves to hurt her.

'I won't let you,' she said. 'I won't let you marry. I will tell...'

'Who would believe you?' he said.

'Angharad must know,' said Elizabeth. 'You know how she watches.'

'And can Angharad tell?' he said.

Then Elizabeth cried.

The morning was cool and so was Betty. Lydia was contrite, not because of her treatment of Finn but because her rejection of him made Betty's kindly presence with her seem not only pointless but rather foolish. She said, 'I do like having you here Betty. You're much nicer than Finn. You don't grunt.'

'Of course I don't grunt,' said Betty. 'Why should I grunt?'

'Finn does,' said Lydia. 'He gets moody

191

and grunts. I used to think he behaved like someone with constant PMT – irrational and unpredictable to an alarming degree. I've often noticed it in men and I've never known a woman to behave as weirdly as a man.'

'Some do,' protested Betty,

'I know some do,' agreed Lydia. 'Some try and hang themselves on lamp-posts outside men's houses, but I don't know any of that sort. The good thing about friends is that you can choose them with consummate care and I never chose mad ones or nasty ones or boring ones, whereas you can't choose who you're going to fall in love with. It just hits you like some spiteful virus and down you go, knowing it's crazy but powerless to resist. There you are with some glum, drunken, disapproving monster and you creep round asking him what's wrong and trying to cheer him up.'

'I can't see you doing that,' said Betty honestly.

'I don't do a lot of it now,' confessed Lydia, 'but I used to. I think I stopped when I once asked someone what the matter was and he said: "If you don't know, then you can't love me." He'd been glaring and smashing down glasses on the table and muttering under his breath and I wondered what on earth I'd done to make him so disturbed, and then I realised I hadn't done anything. It wasn't me at all. It was something at work, or some other woman, or some painful inadequacy he'd discovered in himself, but he was blaming me. That's why women are so much more essential to men than the other way round. Women are more used to accepting the consequences of what they do and accepting their own failings, while men simply must have someone to blame.'

'That's not why you won't have Finn back,' said Betty astutely.

'True,' said Lydia. 'I am sufficiently stupid to have put up with all that for a time, but I will not be cuckolded by a duck. It wouldn't be so bad if he'd gone off with a beauty, but I'm damned if I'll form part of a collection which includes someone bandy.'

'Women can't be cuckolded – and she wasn't bandy,' said Betty.

'Yes, she was,' said Lydia. 'It was because of being web-footed. All ducks are bandy. They waddle.'

'If you insist on being so exclusive,' said Betty, 'you'll never get married.'

'I wouldn't dream of getting married,' said Lydia. 'Why should I get married?'

Betty looked at her uncertainly. Just as Lydia had gradually grown fond of Betty as she recognised her good qualities, so Betty realising how reprehensible Lydia could be liked her less. In the end she would only find her fascinating and feel no pity for her at all. 'Companionship?' she suggested.

'Oh yes,' said Lydia contemptuously, 'and financial security and little children. No thanks.' Mischief had gone to her head and she felt powerful and free and unconstrained. Her plot now seemed more sadly trivial than wicked. If she had known that she would be offered the opportunity of fighting Finn all round the valley, she would never have planned her picnic. She was ashamed of her scheme, now finding it unworthily small-minded.

'If Finn comes back,' she said, 'I'll ask him to the picnic.'

'Why,' asked Betty bluntly, 'if you won't let him stay here and you're so angry with him?'

Lydia was evasive, not having a good answer ready. 'Mmm,' she said shiftily, 'I just thought it might be amusing.'

'For whom?' enquired Betty.

'Oh, for me of course,' said Lydia, forced into the open. 'Don't I deserve any fun?'

'You have lots of fun,' said Betty repressively. 'Too much.'

'I haven't for ages,' pleaded Lydia. 'I've had a terribly peaceful few weeks.'

'You should've asked some of your friends to stay,' said Betty.

'I don't want any of my friends to stay,' said Lydia. 'I'm bored with my friends at the moment.'

Betty looked unhappy. 'I don't think you know what you want,' she said.

'Anyway, I've got you,' said Lydia, rather too late.

Betty smiled in an irritatingly understanding way. 'Oh yes,' she said.

'And Beuno,' added Lydia, rendered unkind by this annoying smile. She wasn't going so far as to make protestations of delight in Betty's company.

'Anyway, I shall have to go back soon,' said Betty. 'You're lucky being freelance. My boss didn't really want me to take three weeks all at once.'

Lydia hadn't thought of that before. She was used to working only when she felt like it, or the deadline loomed too horridly. Besides she had a little money of her own. She wondered when Finn would turn up again. She knew he would.

Elizabeth has left the house. I followed her down the lane on the other side of the hedge. I thought she would cry, but she is angry. I took down the curtains, the pretty curtains that she had made, because they hid my window and made the earth smaller. That wasn't all. I took the milk, and I poured it on the floor where the slate is hollowed, because once I saw the lake in moonlight and it was white. I only saw it once, and I wanted to see it again. I thought if I waited my lake would grow, and if I waited long enough the walls would walk away and the heron would come to swoop above my lake, milk-white in the moonlight. Listen. Elizabeth is angry...

'I don't think I can stand it any more. She's ripped up everything in her bedroom and she's thrown milk all over the kitchen.'

(Only one little, little lake)

'I've tried and tried to look after her well, but she's impossible. I'm sorry to be here like this but I couldn't get through to anyone. The telephone doesn't work...'

(I tore the wire from the wall. It rang while Elizabeth was in the field and I picked it up and someone spoke to me, but I cannot speak, so I tore it from the wall and then no one could speak to me.)

'I'm at my wits' end. She's getting worse and

worse. You know, she follows me sometimes? She's probably outside now, listening. She doesn't understand half of what we say but she listens all the time. I never know where she is.'

(I am here, Elizabeth. Here outside the window.)

'Oh, I am sorry. I shouldn't be here bothering you like this, but she's such a worry. Hiding in corners or out on the hills in all weathers...

(Listen, the little woman is speaking.)

'Oh, Elizabeth, you must worry terribly when she's out.'

(Listen to Elizabeth. Listen, listen, listen.)

All I worry about is that she's going to come back.'

Even Lydia was subdued. She avoided Betty's eye and absent-mindedly put too much sugar in her tea. Finn sat in the armchair eating cake. He had arrived at the precise moment when Elizabeth had begun to sob and then desolately to weep, and all Lydia's skills, social, sexual and manipulative, had abruptly deserted her. She had taken Elizabeth home in the car, leaving Betty to explain to Finn whatever she saw fit.

'There was no one at the farm,' she said. 'I offered to stay, but she obviously wanted me to go. There was a pool of milk in the kitchen but it wasn't too bad. No sign of Beuno. He's as odd as the rest of them really. I think he just dematerialises when he feels like it.'

'He goes for long walks,' said Betty mundanely.

'Who does?' asked Finn.

'Beuno,' said Betty.

'I don't like things with no answer,' said Lydia. 'There doesn't seem to be any answer.'

'Who's Beuno?' asked Finn.

'Oh, do shut up,' said Lydia. 'We're trying to think.' Elizabeth's distress had been so evident that even Lydia felt bound to take it seriously. The game, if game there had been, had broken the constraints of rule, and there is nothing more reminiscent of chaos and old night than a game become uncontrolled. 'Why on earth did she marry him,' she demanded fretfully, 'knowing she'd have Angharad to contend with? She must have had some idea what she was doing.'

'People don't think when they're in love,' said Betty.

'Oh, horsefeathers,' said Lydia crossly, '*I* do.'

Betty, who was obviously getting sick of reminding Lydia that she was unusual, said nothing.

'Who's Angharad?' asked Finn.

'She's Hywel's sister,' said Lydia. 'Do stop asking questions. I hate explaining things. I make my living out of explaining things to a lot of dum-dums, and if I do it at all I expect to get paid.'

'Who's Hywel, Betty?' asked Finn, unperturbed.

'I'll tell you later,' said Betty. 'Lydia, are you sure she was all right to be left alone?'

'No,' said Lydia, 'but she isn't a child and I hardly know her, so I couldn't start throwing my weight around, could I?' Lydia was also faintly disgusted by tears, by the weakness they evinced and by the viscosity of their substance. In truth she now felt guilty for leaving the shuddering Elizabeth alone in the farmhouse. 'I offered to bring her back again but she said she had to wait for Angharad.'

'She must feel terrible for having told us that,' said Betty.

'What?' asked Finn.

'Shut up,' said Lydia. 'Do you suppose Angharad was listening?' she enquired of Betty. 'She does go round very silently. I've seen her but I've never heard her.'

'There was someone outside the kitchen window when I arrived,' said Finn placidly, apparently pleased to be able to contribute something to this limited discussion.

'Oh, help,' said Lydia.

'I wonder how much she *does* understand,' said Betty. To Finn she said, 'I'm sorry I didn't make it very clear. Elizabeth was crying because Angharad's been destroying things in the house.'

Finn said, 'You've done it again, haven't you, Lydia? Landed yourself in the midst of a drama.' And Lydia said, 'If you're going to be rude you can bugger off.' But she said it half-heartedly. The skin was peeling off Finn's nose and she wasn't in love with him any more, so she didn't really care what he did.

Noting the half-heartedness, Finn smiled, misunderstanding. 'I've got to pick up my stuff from the pub,' he said. 'Do you want anything from the village?'

'Cider,' said Betty, 'from the off-licence. We've got everything else.'

'We're having a picnic,' said Lydia wearily. 'Tomorrow. You'll be able to meet all our new friends.'

Betty relaxed. Like Finn, she believed that Lydia had now relented, mistaking her lack of interest for compliance, which led to further misunderstandings at bedtime when Lydia told Finn that he was to sleep in the tiny room where she kept the oil lamps which was furnished with a camp bed and sleeping-bag.

'But...' said Betty.

'But...' said Finn.

'I'm tired,' said Lydia plaintively. When Finn had gone to bed she sat by the fire and looked at the flames.

'What are you doing?' asked Betty in a whisper, coming downstairs in her dressing-gown.

'I'm looking at the fire,' said Lydia. 'If I was a dog you wouldn't let me. You'd tell me I'd go blind.'

'No, I wouldn't,' said Betty.

'Yes, you would,' said Lydia, staring at the flames, lost in thought.

'What are you thinking about?' asked Betty.

'Men,' said Lydia.

'What about them?' asked Betty, settling down for an exchange of confidences, a revelation of Lydia's motives in banishing Finn to the lamp room.

'I was wondering why they talk of possessing women,' said Lydia. 'Do we say that the penny possesses the piggy bank? Or the sausage the roll? Or the jam the sandwich? It seems to me that the foot is in the other boot, so to speak.'

'Oh *Lydia,*' said Betty exasperatedly.

'No,' said Lydia, stirring. 'If ever I catch another man looking at me with that look which means "You're mine, all mine" I shall kill him, because I'm not his all his at all. I think I shall take a vow of perpetual chastity.'

'It's not like that Lydia,' said Betty. 'You know it isn't.'

'Oh, yes it is,' said Lydia.

She sent Beuno to fetch the doctor. She lay in her room and waited for him, and when he came I did not listen, but when he left I heard. He said, 'Until tomorrow,' and she said, very softly, 'Oh love, love.' And when he passed me I did not like to look at his face because it was dark like the shadows of the hill, and when he reached the door he laughed and I did not like to hear him laugh, and when he reached the yard he stopped because Beuno was there and he said to him, 'She'll be all right now. I've given her something and she should rest.'

And Beuno said nothing, but he looked at him as mildly as he looks at the trout that he catches in the stream, and the doctor said, 'Until tomorrow,' and he left, and Beuno watched him go as mildly as he watches the sheep when he frees them from where they are caught in the hedge.

Then he made my supper, and when Hywel came back they talked in Welsh and they laughed.

Elizabeth slept. She is sleeping now. Hywel does not know what I did or how she cried. It is not I but Hywel who is deaf and he has not seen what I have seen.

Finn was very good looking. Lydia realised this afresh when she came downstairs the following morning. He looked at her without animosity and for a moment her knees weakened. He had lovely lines. The line of his neck, decided Lydia, related perfectly to the line of his lower leg with no unsightly discrepancies in between to interrupt this happy progression. She was seeing him sideways on, all profile and flank, and she thought that this was much the pleasantest aspect of all people. Straight on, either front or back, the human being tends to look somewhat banal. This androgynous obliquity of flowing unbroken line was seductive and beautiful.

'Morning, ratface,' she said, quite affectionately because after that momentary frisson she had remembered the duck and known she would never love him again. Because of this she felt generous and said she had realised some time ago that a really beautiful man was very much more beautiful than the most beautiful woman, and wasn't that interesting. Finn said that not being queer he couldn't see that at all, and Lydia, instead of clinging grimly to her theory, agreed that it was probably all in the eye of the beholder. 'What have you done with the duck?' she asked amiably.

'What?' said Finn.

'That awful girl you took to Greece,' explained Lydia.

'Oh, she's around,' said Finn.

'Around where?' asked Lydia.

Finn looked at her speculatively. 'Just around,' he said. 'Does it matter?'

'No,' said Lydia. 'It doesn't. You can make the coffee.'

'We have to talk,' said Finn.

'We are talking,' said Lydia. 'We just had a discussion about aesthetics.'

'You know what I mean,' said Finn.

Lydia did, of course, know what he meant but denied it. 'You can make the toast too,' she said, going into the garden.

Finn followed her. 'I knew at the time it would probably come to nothing,' he said. 'She's completely self-centred. There's nothing to her but...'

Lydia interrupted. It was one thing for *her*

to be rude about a fellow female, quite another for a man. Like all loyalty, loyalty to one's own sex was at once necessary for the survival of the whole and self-serving. Women must protect each other at all costs from the onslaught of the male, particularly from their contempt. Should she permit Finn to speak insultingly of the duck then she would have rendered herself vulnerable; for all traitors are peculiarly at risk – from both within and without.

'*And* she's into women's lib,' added Finn ill-advisedly.

'Good,' said Lydia briskly. 'Splendid. Wonderful. So am I.'

Finn sank further. 'But you're intelligent,' he said. 'You've got a sense of humour.'

'No, I haven't,' said Lydia. 'It wore out a minute or so ago. Don't imagine you can flatter me by telling me I'm not really a feminist, because I *am*, and I find your denials extremely insulting.'

Finn was clearly perplexed. Lydia could see his dilemma. Because he liked women to be gentle and soft and obedient he thought that women would like being that way since it would make him like them. He thought that this was their purpose, their *raison d'être*. He thought all right-minded people of both sexes must hate feminists.

'You see,' said Lydia carefully, 'the only use women have for men is to be impregnated by them. Once they've done that, men can go and boil their heads. They are surplus to requirements.'

Betty in the bathroom could hear every word and could bear it no longer. She leaned out of the open window. 'Oh *Lydia*,' she said, 'you told me only yesterday that you didn't want any children. You know you did.'

'I'm a maverick,' said Lydia. 'I'm the exception that proves the pudding.'

'Oh, you,' said Betty crossly. 'You think you're the light of the world.' She retired into the bathroom with her toothbrush.

'Come here,' said Finn gently, leaning towards Lydia.

He obviously had impregnation on his mind, but by now Lydia had lost her temper and she told him to get stuffed. She apologised later because the atmosphere was getting oppressive. Betty was tight-lipped and Finn was conspicuously sulking.

'Look at him sulking,' she said to Betty, 'he could jump in his car and go to Bogota but no, he's going to sit there and sulk where I can see him.'

'You've hurt him,' said Betty.

Lydia was briefly speechless, but recovered. 'That's exactly the same as telling the wall it's hurt the person who just banged his head on it. Did I ask him to come back? Did I welcome him with open arms? Did I implore him to stay?'

'He's in love with you,' said Betty.

'No, he's not,' said Lydia. 'He's one of those wimps who can't muddle along without a woman and he's gone off the duck so he's come back here.'

'That's not so,' said Betty. 'You're being cruel.'

'I couldn't be cruel to him if he wasn't here, could I?' said Lydia reasonably, but she was beginning to regain her temper. 'I'm sorry,' she said, since the mood of the morning appeared to depend solely on her, and she took Finn a cup of coffee.

The kitchen table was covered with slices of bread and amputated crusts, and Betty was boiling eggs and mashing sardines. A quiche and a cake sat side by side on the dresser veiled with a clean tea-towel.

Lydia thought she should offer to help, but the idea of buttering all those identical pieces of bread made her feel tired. Monotony was exhausting, no matter how light the task with which it was associated. She didn't feel inclined to wrap anything up either. Edible things tended to crumble when packaged and someone was going to have to remember where they all were when the time came to unpack them. She thought it might as well be Betty and sat down by Finn, because then Betty, even if displeased at her laziness, could not fail to commend her courtesy.

'Who exactly are these people you've got coming?' enquired Finn.

'Just some locals,' said Lydia. 'One of them is one of us but the rest are pretty good hell. The situation is rather as though instead of going to the zoo I had invited a small group of creatures to come to me. We have very little in common. I watch them and they watch me, but whereas I feel, possibly mistakenly, that I can comprehend their animal antics, they find me bewilderingly inscrutable.'

'I'm not surprised,' said Finn.

He said it warmly and gently, and at this Lydia was surprised since she had thought her remarks somewhat offensive and would not have made them had she still been in love with Finn and desirous of his good opinion. She looked at him warily to find that he was regarding her with unprecedented tenderness.

'Why are you looking at me like that?' she asked abruptly.

'Like what?' asked Finn.

'Like that,' said Lydia, nearly sticking her finger in his eye. 'As though you found me exceedingly lovable.'

'I do,' said Finn, recoiling, and Lydia thought that here was another ludicrous irony: that the less you were in love with someone the more you could enchant and ensnare them. You could behave like a pig and they would simply think how sweet and original you were, whereas if you were wildly in love you would be on your best behaviour, nervously uncertain and consequently lacking in charm. It was all down to confidence, thought Lydia. The successful artiste is neither timorous nor tremulous but leaps around on the high-wire glittering with outrageous elan and gathering applause.

'It makes you look like a sheep,' she observed coldly, but even this seemed not to offend him. He merely gave her shoulder an affectionate nudge and leaned back on a cushion. Once upon a time, thought Lydia, when I was in love with him, he would've socked me for that. The recollection was faintly depressing, making her realise how little useful or productive communication there had been between them. She wished Beuno was there, standing by the stream and gazing through the alders at the flower-printed meadow.

'They'll be here soon,' she said. 'You'd better help Betty load the stuff in the car.'

Now she began to feel truly depressed, a not uncommon symptom when some social event blithely planned in a moment of cheerfulness becomes threateningly imminent. She wished she could lay claim to a migraine but knew that Betty would not let her, that anyway even she could not be so mannerless as to absent herself from her own picnic, and that even if she did have a blinding migraine she would still have to go. 'Oh, sod,' she said gloomily, getting up.

The Molesworths, all three, arrived with Dr Wyn, who hooted from the lane.

'That's them,' said Betty, picking up little bags of salt, pepper and sugar and peering appraisingly round the kitchen for signs of some forgotten but vital accessory to the meal.

'Oh, come on,' said Lydia. 'Let's get it over with.'

They drove in convoy along the lane to the

farmhouse. The yard was empty. Lydia in the leading car was loth to hoot for fear of maddening the dogs and loth to get out for the same reason.

'Go and bang on the door,' she directed Finn.

'It's all right,' said Betty. 'Wyn's going.'

The dogs snarled and cowered about his ankles. He put his hands on each side of the open door, leaned forward and called: 'Elizabeth.'

He is calling Elizabeth. She stands in the shadow of the stair and then she goes forward. She says, 'Hello, Wyn,' as though they were friends, and steps past him into the yard. She stops at the two cars and then goes to the one with the woman from Ty Fach because the girl is in the other one. I have seen the cats of my country look as she looks now and afterwards make a great howling.

'Well, this is nice,' said Lydia when Elizabeth had got in the back beside Betty.

'I shouldn't really be coming,' said Elizabeth. 'Farmers' wives have no business going on picnics.'

Lydia grew more alert. This was the most interesting thing she had ever heard Elizabeth say, because it had undertones of

211

cynicism, of self-mockery. She reminded herself that it was unlikely that all people could possibly be as stupid as she supposed them to be; that at some level even she, Lydia the clever, could find common ground and communicate intelligibly with other human beings. It was the constraints of formality, the manners and *mores* of different groups that caused alienation. Stripped of mask and domino they were not wholly unlike herself. At one time she had found appalling the comforting observation that people are similar, with much the same fears and fantasies. Not to be unique had seemed to her intolerable, but she was getting more sensible. Humbly she said what was expected of her, made the appropriate response. 'You must have a change sometimes,' she said. 'All work and no play...'

Finn glanced at her suspiciously.

'No, really,' said Lydia.

She had driven as far as she could and now stopped the car.

The doctor drew up and parked beside her and everyone got out. Several people complimented her on the beauty of the surroundings, because it was her picnic and so for a while Wales was her dining room.

'Where's Beuno?' asked Betty casually,

and Lydia realised that she must have been silently asking that all the way from the farmhouse. She looked enquiringly at Elizabeth.

'He said he'd meet us here,' said Elizabeth. 'He likes to walk.'

April suddenly began to behave very badly. She draped herself round the doctor and adopted a childish air.

He responded by calling her darling rather more often than was natural.

Her parents looked on indulgently. 'Lovely bit of weather,' said her father, and her mother remarked that she always thought it so silly of them not to go out in the country more when they lived so near to it.

'We've got to walk a bit now,' said Lydia.

'But it's so pretty here,' said April's Mum.

'Shouldn't we wait for Beuno?' said Betty.

Lydia said that ever since running-boards had gone from cars only very vulgar people ate their victuals in the vicinity of their vehicles.

The extreme snobbery of this abstruse observation would have been rude had it been clear, for Lydia knew perfectly well that the Molesworths were the sort of people who picnicked in lay-bys, bringing little chairs and tables and using the car boot as a sort of sideboard.

'We must all carry something,' she said, 'and make safari.'

Betty noticed however that Lydia contrived to carry nothing but a bottle of cider which she had clearly earmarked for herself.

Lydia led the way, conspicuous in red linen. She went in the opposite direction from the rock drawings, her planned destination when she had first conceived her scheme. How, she wondered bemusedly, could she have been so trivial recently as to wish to upset these unexceptionable people.

Finn caught up with her and she stopped, turning round to gauge her following. 'Wait for Elizabeth,' she commanded him. 'Walk with her.'

Elizabeth was walking with Betty behind the doctor and April, who was clinging to his arm and, as it were, daintily tripping up. She probably imagined she was comporting herself in an attractively provocative and feminine fashion, thought Lydia, sneering and lengthening her stride.

'She's walking with Betty,' said Finn.

'Exactly,' said Lydia.

'What?' said Finn.

'What do you mean "What?"' said Lydia.

'I don't know what you're talking about,'

said Finn.

'You're stupid,' said Lydia. 'She's in love with that creepy doctor and he's flashing that dreary April around to upset her. Can't you see?'

'Nonsense,' said Finn, who was, like most heterosexual men, disarmingly simple-minded in these matters. 'You're imagining things.'

Lydia was so annoyed at this that she couldn't think where to begin but promised herself that Finn should suffer for his insolence.

They had reached a stretch of mountain where the ground was comparatively parallel with the sky. 'This will do,' she said. 'I can't bear picnicking on a slope. All the buns go rolling away.'

Beuno was sitting by a deep pool which the flatness of the ground had permitted the stream to form.

'And here is lovely Beuno,' said Lydia. 'He is studying for the ministry. How clever he is to know where we should find him.'

She looked sideways at Finn to see if he was sufficiently irritated by all this. He was. He banged down the rucksack and the basket he had been carrying and looked without liking at the unencumbered Beuno.

There was fortunately no wind at all. The tablecloth needed no stones to hold it down and all the plastic bags waited for Betty to put them in the master plastic bag she had brought for the purpose. The sun shone with magisterial tranquillity and the few clouds kept their distance from it.

'What a lovely day,' said Mrs Molesworth when she had got her breath back. 'April, make sure you sit on a blanket.'

For a while there was no conversation and Lydia began to regret that she had put Finn in a bad mood, since usually he was prepared to entertain when she was not.

'I'm glad they haven't started planting conifers up here,' she remarked at last, resignedly and in a monotonous tone.

'Yes,' agreed the doctor, 'they quite alter the ecology.'

'They do offer job opportunities to the locals,' said Mr Molesworth.

'I think they're rather pretty,' said Mrs Molesworth. 'All those little Christmas trees.'

'They smell nice,' said April unexpectedly, 'like cough mixture.' She giggled and snuggled closer to her lover.

'The rain forests are being dreadfully depleted,' said Betty.

'Dutch elm disease is a terrible thing,' said

Mr Molesworth, coming round for a second time.

'Something like 90,000 acres of trees per minute are being chopped down all over the world;' contributed Lydia off the top of her head.

They looked at her doubtfully.

'How long does it take a conifer to grow to a size where it can be used?' she asked hastily, since her last remark had threatened to take the discussion off course. 'Come to think of it,' she added with more interest, 'what do they use them for? Pit props? Paper? All that poxy pine furniture people keep buying?'

'They have a lot of purposes,' said Mr Molesworth, who clearly didn't know.

But now Betty came to the rescue and began to unpack the sardine sandwiches.

They are sitting by the eye of the stream where it looks up at the sun before it weeps down the mountainside. I am above them, so high I hear the small birds sing below me. So high that I cannot hear them speak. Elizabeth will not speak. If she spoke she would say, 'Wyn, Wyn, Wyn...'

'Come for a healthy walk then, lazybones,'

said the doctor, hauling April to her feet. Whereupon she said, 'Eeeee–' – in a high-pitched, slaughtered-pig-like way, thought Lydia, eyeing her dispassionately. April dipped her fingers into a paper cup of cider and flicked it at him before skipping away uphill.

'Preserve us,' said Lydia aloud, turning on to her side.

Mrs Molesworth was paddling and her husband was poking at the stones because, he said, fossils were one of his hobbies.

'You've certainly got an odd collection here,' said Finn. 'Who's the poof?'

'He's not a poof,' said Lydia carefully.

'Oh, come on,' said Finn, 'I've been talking to Betty. She says he's never going to get married.'

'Neither am I,' said Lydia, 'and *I'm* not a poof. Anyway, if you've been talking to Betty you know who he is.'

She was pleased with the way things were turning out. Betty would have spoken well and warmly of Beuno, and Finn was clearly jealous.

'*Ministry,*' continued Finn with contempt. '*Celibate.*'

'He's in love with God,' said Lydia, rolling on to her back and staring at the sky. 'I can't *tell* you how boring people look once you've fallen in love with God.'

'And what would *you* know about that?' enquired Finn.

Lydia was silent.

'Come on,' said Finn, beginning to get nasty. 'What do *you* know about the love of God?'

But Lydia had discovered, to her own surprise, that she found the matter too significant to quarrel about in a childish way. If she was going to quarrel about it at all she would have to do it seriously. 'Betty wants to marry him,' she said. 'That's why she was talking about marriage.'

'You're such a fantasist, Lydia,' said Finn, predictably.

This Lydia *was* prepared to quarrel about. 'Do you mean that in your opinion Betty doesn't want to get married?' she asked. 'Or do you mean she doesn't want to marry Beuno? Because I can assure you that you are entirely wrong on both counts.'

'Nonsense,' said Finn, and Lydia decided that even had he not gone off with the duck their relationship would have had no future.

I can only see them, but I can see them all. Only Beuno knows I am here. Beuno has always

219

known where I am. I have seen what they call love and heard them speak of it. What Beuno feels for me is not what they feel for each other. Perhaps it is love. I cannot tell. I can see him across the wide air looking at where I am and if he was closer he would look into my eyes. No one else looks into my eyes.

'Hell,' said Lydia, starting up. She had just noticed the direction that the doctor was taking, April jigging along beside him. 'Gripes. Finn, make them come back.'

'What's wrong now?' said Finn, his voice coloured by laziness and ill-temper.

'Oh lawks,' said Lydia agitatedly. 'Hell and damnation.'

'What *is* it?' said Finn.

'It's too late,' said Lydia, lying back on the grass and manifesting despair. 'Oh well, who cares.'

She had seen, in the distance, the doctor and April making unerringly for the cave-like depression which contained the rock drawings and would indeed offer a splendid location for a spot of slap-and-tickle. The same thought might have occurred to Mrs Molesworth, because she was heading after them.

'Dear, oh bloody dear,' said Lydia, sitting

220

up in renewed dismay, but they had turned and were coming downhill. 'It could've been worse,' she said.

Finn still had no idea what she was talking about and was not at all interested anyway.

'Well, *you* certainly don't care,' said Lydia, irrationally annoyed. As well as being rather stupid, Finn now had grass in his hair and was looking rather stupid. One of the worst things about falling in love was falling out again, taking a long clear look at the erstwhile beloved and feeling a total lemon. It was a sensation Lydia cordially resented.

'Had a nice walk?' she asked coldly as the doctor came level.

'Lovely,' said April. 'We saw some...'

The doctor knocked over a bottle of cider and Lydia leapt too late to save it, as it shattered against a flat stone. He was in a terrible temper. He was white, and several of those muscles with which the human face is so richly endowed and which are seldom called into play in a civilised context were working at the sides of his nose, pulling at his upper lip.

'Darling, you are snarling,' whispered Lydia to the cider bottle.

'You go too fast,' complained Mrs Molesworth, panting to a halt.

Lydia felt quite sorry for the doctor, who so clearly wanted to kick hell out of someone and could find no excuse. April clung to his jacket sleeve being winsome: very unwisely in Lydia's opinion.

'We'll have to be starting back soon,' she said mercifully.

He saw me. He stepped back and looked up, and his eyes saw my eyes. I thought it is good that I am dead, and good that Hywel is standing on the mountainside to the north, and good that Beuno is sitting on the mountainside to the south, and good that the girl is there, laughing, because his face was the face of the fox in the trap and if we had been alone his face would have been the face of the fox in freedom alone with the hare on the mountainside.

'When I was a little girl,' said Lydia, 'a dear little curly-headed girl, I used to keep bunnies, dear little furry bunnies, and when I shut them in for the night – that is when I remembered to shut them in for the night – I always used to wonder what they did when I wasn't watching them. Sometimes they were eating their babies.'

'Oh, don't,' said Betty in distress.

'So that was how I knew they went on

existing when I wasn't watching them,' said Lydia.

'Are you wondering what will happen to the people of the valley when you go away?' asked Beuno.

'Yes, of course,' said Lydia.

'They will go on eating their babies,' said Beuno. 'But most of them will be here when you come back.'

'What do they do when *you're* not watching them?' asked Lydia.

'Much the same as what they do when *you're* not watching them,' he said. 'But I'm one of them, so I know what they do, and even when I'm away the things that I do are the same as the things that I did and the same as the things that they're doing.'

Betty looked bewildered, so Lydia explained. 'Ants,' she said, 'always behave in much the same way, so when an ant is absent he knows very deeply what the other ants are doing, while you and me are – say – grasshoppers, so when we're not watching ants we don't know what they're doing.'

Betty looked more bewildered. 'I hope Elizabeth's all right,' she said, trying to bring some sense back to the evening.

Elizabeth had trodden on the broken cider bottle and a fierce shard of glass had cut the side of her foot, causing a great deal of blood to flow and making Lydia feel ill. The strange thing was that the doctor had insisted on taking her back to the farmhouse, telling Mr Molesworth to drive home his wife and disgruntled daughter. 'How will you get back for surgery?' April had asked, her suspicion making this innocent question sound like an accusation, and Lydia had said, 'I'll take him,' and April had hated her again.

Now Lydia was waiting for him to walk down the lane from the farmhouse, and while she waited she half-expected to hear a shot, or a number of shots, depending on who had shot whom: one if it was him shooting in the cold rage of the threatened libertine, and several if it was her taking boss-eyed and vengeful shots at a faithless lover. On the other hand, reflected Lydia, considering the nature of his calling he could merely put some deleterious substance in the wound and watch the wretched woman slowly die, while she could poison the Welsh cake which she might offer him for tea.

Finn was making a pot of coffee and wondering why Beuno didn't go home. Lydia could see him willing this as he reluctantly got four mugs from the dresser, but Beuno was as untroubled as a cat in the presence of a cat hater.

'I could never love a doctor,' said Lydia, thinking aloud, 'because one's person would hold no mystery for him.'

'Elizabeth will soon be better,' said Beuno, and now Finn looked bewildered.

'Do you think so?' asked Lydia, leaving her doubts unsaid.

'Oh, yes, I think so,' said Beuno.

'She's only got a cut foot,' said Finn, driven by exasperation into contributing to this odd conversation with its gaping spaces of meaning.

'Then Stan can return to the pit,' said Lydia comfortably, ignoring Finn.

'The holidays are over,' said Betty suddenly. 'Do you realise I must be back by the day after tomorrow?'

'I'll drive you,' said Finn. 'I have to get back too.'

Lydia was shocked by this, but only slightly. Betty and Finn? Finn and Betty? Well, why not? Betty was an improvement on the duck.

'Bless you, my children,' she said smiling knowingly and thereby strangling at birth the infant possibility of a new love affair. She saw at once what she had done and on the whole was glad. She would not really have liked to see Betty wearing her old clothes nor, by the same token, arm in arm with her old love.

She prattled as she drove the doctor back to his place of work because she was wondering what it must be like to dress the wounded foot of a discarded mistress and had forbidden herself to ask.

'You'll be going soon then,' he said.

'Yes,' said Lydia, 'but I'll be back.' She didn't care if he thought of her as an outsider. Beuno didn't.

Yet as she returned she was overcome by a feeling of such desolation that Lydia, who never wept, thought that tears might gush from her eyes with so great a force that they would wash the windscreen. She didn't know where she belonged.

She said so to Beuno, who was waiting for her in the cow parsley by the lane. She leaned out of the car window and told him.

'With God,' said Beuno placidly, 'that sense of homelessness is a reminder of where you belong.'

'Some would say it was a yearning to get back to the womb,' said Lydia.

'Some would say anything,' said Beuno.

'How fortunate it is,' said Lydia, 'in view of your proposed way of life, that you believe in God. How boring for you it would be if you

226

didn't.' She heard undertones of jealousy in her remark and hastened to apologise. 'I believe in God myself,' she explained, 'but on the whole this belief inconveniences rather than supports me. It makes me feel inadequate and toad-like when I would prefer to feel rather wonderful and extremely happy. I wonder what happened to the laughter.'

'I exorcised it,' said Beuno.

Lydia was suddenly annoyed with him. 'It was *my* laughter,' she said. 'You might've asked. Exorcising people's laughter without asking them!'

Beuno looked at her with the expression of someone watching a normally reasonable person behaving irrationally and waiting for him to return to his senses.

Lydia read this look immediately because it was unmistakable: a look worn only by those in authority, since no one else has the right to wait in expectation of an instant change in demeanour on the part of another.

'Oh, all right,' she said, 'it wasn't my laughter at all. It was the valley's laughter, so I suppose it was more yours than mine anyway.'

'No,' said Beuno, 'it is possible that you brought it with you. I just didn't think it advisable to let it persist. It's the same instinct as that which causes me to turn off a dripping tap whoever it belongs to.'

'Yes, I know,' said Lydia. 'Like things out of place. The secret behind surrealism. It gives you a bit of a turn, but then you realise how essentially childish it is, and somehow dangerous.'

'Children *have* a sense of order, of propriety, but haven't yet understood quite where things should be. Like Angharad and the milk.' He looked across the fields.

Lydia had the impression that he was about to give her as a farewell present either a benediction or a confidence, and that which was most wilful and contrary in her nature rose to refuse it. 'Got to dash now,' she said in a light, social tone she had not previously used with Beuno. 'See you next hols.'

They think that death is waiting at the end of the ride, that life is like the lane and that death waits at the end. Listen. That is death on the other side of the hedgerow. And that swift shadow that is gone, before you turn, from the corner of your eye – that is death. And the whisper you can scarcely hear through the sounds of the birds calling and the wind in the leaves that is death. Not waiting, but there beside you within reach, within earshot, so close that if you should look you would see your breath cloud on his presence. There he is, just out of sight behind the wild rose and the black-thorn, not behind you, nor before you, but beside you – and he keeps in step. Run, run, run and he will run with you. Or sit weeping on the grass by the lane and he will sit with you, not weeping. I know him well.

Elizabeth saw death today in the eyes of the doctor, and he, looking up, saw death in her eyes. She said, 'It's over, isn't it?'

And he said, 'It's been over for a long time, Elizabeth.' He was gentle with her wounded foot, but I could hear him smiling.

She said, 'What shall I do?'

And he said, 'You'll live, Elizabeth.'

She said, 'I wish I was dead.'

'I have a perfectly horrible sense of mortality,' said Lydia.

'It probably comes from living next door to a graveyard,' said Betty.

'I don't have it in the graveyard,' said Lydia. 'There is a pleasant sense of consummation in the graveyard. No one's going anywhere. Travelling always makes me think of death. Packing up to leave makes me feel like my own relict going through things that I have no further use for. When I remove my enlivening presence from this house it will be as though the house had died. Poor little house.' A melancholy tear clung briefly to her eyelashes.

'I don't believe I've ever known you sentimental before,' said Betty wonderingly.

'I've changed,' said Lydia. 'I've never stayed here as long before, nor met any of the people really, and now I'm all undone. I don't know whether I'm sad because I'm sorry for them staying here, or sad because I'm not staying here, or sad because I ever came here in the first place, or whether I'm merely suffering from softening of the brain brought on by mixing with my intellectual inferiors.'

This sounded more like the old Lydia. 'You've done nothing for weeks but tell me how intelligent the people here are,' accused Betty.

'I'm thinking of the Molesworths,' explained Lydia. 'They make me feel as though I'd been watching television advertisements or reading women's magazines.'

'You've written for women's magazines yourself,' said Betty.

'Only cleverly,' protested Lydia. 'Only about large and important issues.'

'Is she showing off again?' asked Finn,

diverted from the newspaper by this conceited remark.

'Yes, she is,' said Betty.

Lydia understood that, for the moment at least, she was friendless; had managed to either offend or alienate all those in her immediate circle. How she now regretted her airy dismissal of Beuno, the only friend she possessed who was worthy of respect and had reached a peak of maturity from which he would not stoop to tease. Betty and Finn were both displeased with her and united in their determination to bring her down a peg or two. They were closing in for the kill. 'You'd wonder what she had to be quite so conceited about, wouldn't you?' That was Finn, laying down his paper and regarding her speculatively. He was offended because he was beginning to realise that Lydia no longer loved him. This inconceivable state of affairs was causing him to regress. It is the frustration of sexual immaturity which makes little boys pull the plaits of little girls and spitefully pinch them. Finn was beginning to remind her of the doctor.

'You just watch it,' she said extremely aggressively.

'Oh dear,' said Betty in mock alarm. 'She's going to get angry.'

The alarm became real as Lydia rounded on her.

Lydia forced herself to be calm, refusing to be drawn into a playground rough-house. 'You should get moving if you want to miss the traffic the other end,' she advised them without interest or rancour – the big girl who will not squabble or submit to silly games. It was very irritating for Betty and Finn who were both half-conscious of the atmosphere and of what was causing it, and who both knew that actually Lydia was the least responsible person present. Her grown-up airs were annoying.

'Yes, I suppose so,' said Betty resignedly. She was longing to tell Lydia a few home truths, but now was not the moment. Well-brought-up people don't accuse their hostess of selfishness, vanity and heartlessness as they depart. They thank her very much and say what a wonderful time they've had.

As they stood by Finn's car Lydia's ill-temper left her. 'It was lovely having you here,' she said to Betty and she meant it. It was these occasional impulses of costless generosity which made people love the undeserving Lydia. 'You must come again *soon*,' she added and she meant that too. Betty was utterly disarmed.

'Goodbye Finn, my petal. Be very good,' said Lydia to her erstwhile love. She was feeling quite fond of him too now that he was getting into his car. Despite the un-doubted sincerity of her parting affection she grinned foxily to herself as she walked back to her cottage since she knew that Betty would now refuse to discuss her shortcom-ings on the journey home. Finn who would have been soothed to hear Betty assuring him that Lydia was self-centred, ungrateful and capricious would now have to forgo that pleasure because Lydia had, at the last moment, laid claim to Betty's absolute allegiance.

The cottage felt different now that she was alone. She washed up the dishes that her guests had used and tidied things away until she had removed all trace of their presence. Last night Betty had urged her to return with them, worrying that Lydia would be nervous and lonely when they had gone, but Lydia had said she wanted just one more night to finish the article to which she had intended to dedicate a whole week and Finn had nagged her about her laziness and irresponsibility, which had made her cross. Although true, it was unjust, because somehow she had always met her deadlines, and had already in effect finished the article in question.

She enjoyed her last day. She liked lying alone in the sun and going into the cool shadow of a totally tidy cottage, and she liked the silence. She had forgotten how whole silence was, how voices and movement could crack and disfigure it.

She was disconcerted to hear a car stop in the lane and then to see the doctor crossing the stream.

He said, 'I thought you'd gone, but I saw the other two buying petrol in the village and they said you were still here.'

'I had to stay and work,' said Lydia who was flanked on the one hand by a paperback thriller and on the other by a glass and bottle of vodka.

He seemed not to notice. He was a worried man. It occurred to Lydia that he was afraid that she was going to write about him, an exposure of a well-liked and respected country GP. It was a not uncommon neurosis. Lydia had often noticed people urgently wishing that they hadn't said that last thing which would look so damning in print, but she almost never named names and the people about whom she wrote frequently failed to recognise themselves, since Lydia was not a true voyeur, being largely uninterested in her raw material and more concerned with the shape and patina of the finished article.

'You going to write about us all then?' he asked, to her gratification. She wished that Betty had been here, that she had whispered to Betty that she knew what was troubling him, that Betty had heard this swift confirmation of Lydia's insight.

'Gosh no,' she said with offensive surprise, her eyebrows raised – implying, what on earth could I find to write about in this dead-and-alive backwater with its dead-and-alive inhabitants? 'Something would have to happen. Some fearful scandal culminating in murder. You murder someone and I promise I shall come and write all about it.'

Was it her imagination or did he look suddenly aghast? Had she hit some unseen nail on the head?

'Well, I must get on now,' he said after a pause. 'We'll be seeing you again?'

'Of course,' said Lydia, but when he had gone and it was silent she pictured the garden, the cottage lying empty, the hearth cold, the faint dust undisturbed, and her projected return seemed for a moment like an act of violence. I must think of myself more as a migrant bird, she told herself, more like a swallow than an invader. I do not, after all, come in my caravan with my dinghy strapped to the top, strewing crisp packets amongst the sedge by the lake. I do not wear an orange anorak, or bring my young to lay waste the countryside. Just as the swallow, I shall return each year to this nesting place – and sod them if they don't like it. But the sorrow was there still, the sorrow of not belonging. She determined that when she died she would be buried in the graveyard here, and then let them try to distinguish her dust from the dust of the district.

Lydia locked the door, almost in tears with the misery of departure. She got into her car and drove out of Wales. Her spirits were rising. She sang a little song. It was a long time since she had seen her friends. She thought that as soon as she got back to London she would give a party and have a good laugh.

They have gone. The winter will come soon. I wish I was flying now. The silence is unbroken.
  Listen.

The publishers hope that this book has given you enjoyable reading. Large Print Books are especially designed to be as easy to see and hold as possible. If you wish a complete list of our books please ask at your local library or write directly to:

Magna Large Print Books
Magna House, Long Preston,
Skipton, North Yorkshire.
BD23 4ND

This Large Print Book, for people
who cannot read normal print,
is published under the auspices of

THE ULVERSCROFT FOUNDATION

MAA.